PLEASE SEND SIX BRIDES TO DANIEL EDMONDS IN SALT LAKE CITY, UTAH, USA. STOP. ALL MUST BE VIRGINS. THEY MUST BE ACCOMPANIED ACROSS THE COUNTRY BY A RESPONSIBLE FEMALE GUARDIAN WHO WILL ATTEST TO THEIR VIRTUE UPON ARRIVAL.

"These girls are beautiful," Raider said.

Agnes, the guardian, reminded Raider. "You'd be better off not looking. I can promise you, you'll just be wasting your time."

"Yup, I reckon I would." Raider answered . . . but it wasn't what he was thinking. . .

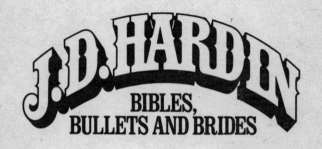

J.D. HARDIN

BIBLES, BULLETS AND BRIDES

BERKLEY BOOKS, NEW YORK

BIBLES, BULLETS AND BRIDES

A Berkley Book / published by arrangement with
the author

PRINTING HISTORY
Berkley edition / March 1983

ISBN: 0-425-06001-2

PRINTED IN THE UNITED STATES OF AMERICA

CHAPTER ONE

Middletown, on New York's Long Island, was not exactly Raider's idea of utopia. He'd spent the last week of a month's vacation in New York City, where there had been enough liquor and pretty girls to make him think that the Northeast wasn't so bad, after all. Middletown, on the other hand, reassured him that a man was out of his mind to cross the Mississippi River and the Mason-Dixon line.

Middletown was the sleepiest place Raider had landed in since joining the Pinkerton agency. Located in the center of Long Island, it offered few diversions other than farming and fishing. After a four-and-a-half-week absence from Pinkerton, he was itching for something more exciting.

Fortunately, his stay in Middletown would be short. Wagner, his Pinkerton connection in Chicago, had instructed Raider to go to a town called Roslyn and meet a boat there. He was then to ensure that the boat's cargo arrived safely in Salt Lake City, Utah, whatever that cargo might be.

It was just after eight o'clock in the morning, and he was supposed to be in Roslyn by ten-thirty. He pulled on his Stetson and descended the stairs of the Noon Inn,

Middletown's only hotel. There was a small dining room to the right where Mr. and Mrs. Noon, the innkeepers, were busy serving breakfast to the only other guest. As Raider appeared in the doorway, all heads turned. Although they'd seen him the previous day when he'd arrived, they were still awed by his appearance this morning. Six feet two inches tall and lean, he had the look of a man who'd logged plenty of time in the saddle. A rawhide-tough face was dominated by a sinister black moustache and striking black eyes. A thin waist rose into broad shoulders and powerful arms. His black Stetson, denims, and disreputable-looking leather jacket caused Raider to stand out like a sore thumb from the collection of farmboys who populated the small town.

"Oh, Mr. Raider," said Mrs. Noon, "pardon our rudeness. Please be seated and I'll have your breakfast ready in no time."

She scurried off nervously as Raider sat across from the other guest, a fat, balding man in a black suit and shoestring tie. Raider removed his hat and put it on the table next to his plate. He glanced up at his table companion, who was shoveling scrambled eggs into his mouth, and then looked down at his plate and knew that he wanted nothing more than to eat his breakfast and get out of Middletown.

Mrs. Noon returned, forced a smile, and served Raider scrambled eggs, bacon, and fresh sausage. She poured him a cup of coffee and then joined her husband for their breakfast. Raider took his hat from the table and put it on the floor.

"I don't suppose you're from around here," said Mr. Noon.

"No," Raider answered, "I'm not."

"West?"

"I was born down in Arkansas. Been moving around a lot lately."

"You a farmer?"

"No," Raider said, laughing. "I just do a little of this, a little of that. Mostly, I punch cows."

"No ranches around here," Mr. Noon said as he sipped from his cup. "Just farming and fishing."

"I don't plan on staying. Just visiting some folks I know in Roslyn. Is it far?"

"A few miles north. You'll make it in an hour."

Raider glanced over at the fat man who was still occupied with his meal.

"Then you won't be staying with us tonight, Mr. Raider?" Mrs. Noon asked.

"No, ma'am. I do have to be moving on after breakfast."

"What a shame," she said, casting a relieved look in her husband's direction.

Raider finished his meal, got his belongings together, and left the dining room. There was a taproom directly across the hall, but he resisted the temptation to ask for a shot of bourbon to make his stay on Long Island more bearable. He paid his bill, left the hotel with a nod to the Noons, and rode off on his horse, a mottled gelding. He glanced briefly at the travel instructions Mr. Noon had written out for him and then shoved them in his pocket and turned his attention to the scenery. Long Island seemed to be a beautiful place, filled with dozens of streams winding around wooden houses and small farms. He heard cows and chickens and saw draft horses being tacked up to work in the fields.

After about an hour of traveling, Raider realized that he had drifted off course. He kicked the horse in the girth and rode a little faster. He'd seen some fisherman heading that way earlier and figured that the water must be in that direction.

He reached a harbor but didn't see any people who looked like they were expecting him. He rode down to the shore and asked a man, "What's the name of this here harbor?"

The fisherman, who was boarding a sloop, looked at Raider incredulously. "This here is Port Washington Harbor, cowboy."

"Damn it," said Raider, slapping his leg, "am I far from Roslyn?"

"Nope. Just ride along the shore and you'll be there in half an hour."

"Good," Raider said. "What time is it?"

The man pulled an open-faced gold pocket watch from his jacket and looked at it. "About half past ten," he said.

"Thanks." Raider turned and rode in the direction the man had indicated. He brought the horse to a trot, hoping to reach Roslyn before it was too late.

By the time he got there, the harbor was nearly empty. Most of the fishing boats were already out to sea. A hundred yards to his right was a large covered wagon on which a gray-haired woman held the reins to two huge, gray Percheron draft horses. Raider slowly approached the wagon from behind. The woman heard him and glanced over her shoulder.

"Well," she said in a loud, raspy voice, "it ain't too hard to tell that you're Mr. Raider. You're probably the only cowboy within a thousand miles of here."

"Yeah, I'm Raider," he said. "Who are you?"

"Griffin. Agnes Griffin."

"Well, can you tell me where the cargo is?"

"Listen, Mr. Raider, if you'd been here at ten-thirty when you were supposed to be, I would have told you where the cargo was. But it ain't ten-thirty; it's after eleven, and the cargo is safely packed in this wagon. I'd suggest we move out. It's a long way to Salt Lake City."

"Just a dang minute," Raider shouted. "You ain't going nowhere. My orders said nothing about no old woman."

"Suit yourself," she said, "but no old woman, no cargo. Those are *my* orders, and it's as simple as that."

Raider rubbed his eyes and then spat. He said in as reasonable a voice as he could muster, "This is a tough trip, lady. We're heading out west. I don't know what we're hauling, but you can bet somebody out there wants it, and people out there usually try and take what they want. I don't mean farmboys like you got around here. I mean gunslingers, outlaws, bad hombres."

Agnes laughed. She said, "Listen, cowboy, I was living in Oklahoma when you was in a cradle and in Oregon when you was learning to read, if you ever did. I crossed this country more times than you crossed the road, so if you want this cargo, let's go. Otherwise, I'll take it and the fee for myself."

"Okay, lady," he said, "but I don't like it."

Agnes Griffin slapped the team of horses lightly on the back, and they lurched forward. Raider dropped back until he was abreast of the covered wagon. He studied its driver. Agnes had a square build with thick arms and legs. Her gray hair was pulled back in a bun and framed a rugged yet youthful face. A blue checkered dress did little to hide her stout figure and huge stomach.

She noticed his stares and asked, "How old?"

"Huh?"

"How old do you figure I am? I seen you looking. Take a guess."

Despite her unappealing appearance, her face made her look young.

"Fifty," said Raider. Actually, he thought that forty-five would have been more accurate, but he didn't want to give her the satisfaction.

"You're closer than most," she said. "I been fifty-nine since February."

Raider tried not to look impressed. "Great," he said. "I get to play nursemaid to an old lady clear across the country."

"We'll see who plays nursemaid to who," she said.

"I just hope I don't get killed because of this."

"That makes two of us."

They rode along silently for a few minutes before Raider said, "We'll be staying in New York tonight, but in a couple of days we'll be heading into tougher country. Any complaints and I'll leave you behind, no matter where we are."

She looked into his scowling face and smiled. "Sonny," she said, "I can go a week without water. I can shoot the core out of an apple at fifty paces. I got lots of brains and, goodness knows, plenty of brawn. If we get into a scrape, I promise you, you won't have to worry none about me."

Somehow, Raider believed her. Still, he was uncomfortable traveling with an old woman, felt inhibited by her presence. On top of it, he didn't like her. She rubbed him the wrong way.

"What are we hauling, anyway?" he asked. "They never did tell me that."

"Some m.o.b.'s from England."

Raider's expression reflected his lack of understanding.

"What's the matter?" Agnes asked. "You never hauled m.o.b.'s before?"

"Of course I have," he said, not wanting to admit his ignorance. "I've hauled plenty of them."

"Good," she said. "I don't want to end up teaching no novice."

"There ain't nothing you can teach me that I don't already know."

"Maybe not," she said, looking directly into his eyes,

"but I bet I could have taught you plenty a few years ago. I reckon I might have enjoyed the lesson, too."

Raider was embarrassed by the remark and pulled out in front of the wagon.

"What's the matter, sonny?" Agnes called after him. "You don't like old ladies flirting with you? I don't blame you none, but there ain't nothing to worry about anymore. I'm afraid I'm all bark these days. Too bad I didn't meet you while I was still biting."

Raider continued riding in front of the wagon.

"Listen, sonny," Agnes shouted. "Like it or not, we're together for the next two thousand miles. You might as well come back here and talk to me."

"Somebody's got to scout ahead. What do you think I'm getting paid for?"

"The biggest crime in this here town's history was probably when some six-year-old stole a string of licorice from the general store. I figure we'll be safe for a spell."

Raider laughed and dropped back next to the wagon.

"See?" she said. "I ain't so bad, am I?"

The large covered wagon drew stares from everybody it passed. People on Long Island weren't used to seeing an old lady driving a wagon that had been out of date for many years.

"You ever been to New York City?" Agnes asked Raider.

"Spent a week there once. I can't say I like big cities much. I need room, if you know what I mean."

"I reckon I do. I was there about twenty years ago. Probably changed."

"You'll see for yourself soon enough, lady."

By early afternoon, the temperature had reached into the low eighties. Raider was accustomed to the arid climate of the West, and the sweat caused his white shirt to cling to his back. Beads of perspiration poured off his sideburns and moustache. He removed his hat and mopped his brow with a rumpled red handkerchief.

"Sure is hot," he said.

"It ain't the heat, sonny, it's the humidity. You ain't been around enough water."

"I guess not. Seems like everywhere you look around here, there's a stream or a pond or something. I'll try to remember it next time I'm passing through Arizona."

"Wait till you get a look at the old Salt Lake itself. It's a sight you won't soon forget. Just make sure you don't get a mind to drink any of it. They don't call it Salt Lake for nothing."

By early evening they'd reached Manhattan and were looking for the hotel at which Wagner had instructed Raider to stay. Raider hadn't the slightest idea how to go about finding it, and Agnes just sat with her mouth wide open as she observed the stream of horse-drawn streetcars, rockaway surreys, and other carriages that passed them—and, of course, the throngs of people.

"Even I ain't never seen anything as crazy as this place," she said. "How in the hell are folks supposed to live?"

"Let's just worry about finding our hotel," said Raider. "It'll be getting dark soon."

They asked several people before finding someone who told them that the White Stag Hotel was on the other side of town. They followed his directions and continued to draw attention every inch of the way: a stout frontier woman at the reins of an antique wagon and a raw, lean cowboy on horseback at her side. Finally, they pulled up in front of the hotel.

"I'm glad we finally found this place," Raider said. "I'm used to towns where all you got to do is drive down Main Street and find everything you want. Every damn road here looks like Main Street."

"Ain't that the truth," said Agnes. "You like it better?"

"Nah, but Doc would."

"Who?"

"Doc Weatherbee, my partner."

"With Pinkerton?"

"Yup."

"How come he ain't with you this trip?"

"That's a good question, lady. He'd be having the time of his life around here. He's always telling me about New York and places like that, but after seeing it, I'll take Arkansas any day."

"How does a cowboy like you manage to get along with a city boy like this Doc fellow?"

"Well, as riled up as that city slicker can make me, there's nobody in the world I'd rather team with. He knows what I'm thinking even before I do, and more than once he's gotten me out of a tough spot."

"I'll try to live up to what you're used to," she said.

"Just don't turn city slicker on me." He smiled for the first time since meeting her.

She climbed down from the wagon and looked up at the hotel, with her leathery hands on her stout hips. "As much as I hate to admit it, sonny," she said, "I'm glad you'll be around tonight. I always get the willies when I'm close to this many people."

"Hold on a minute," Raider snapped. "We got a deal. No crying for help or I leave you behind. No offense, Agnes, but you might be the only woman I see for a spell. As long as I got me a city full of whiskey and women, I'm heading out to see what I can rustle up."

Agnes laughed heartily. "You don't understand, cowboy. I'm not the one who needs you. It's the cargo."

"What the hell are you talking about? We'll leave the cargo in the livery stable."

"Not with six hotel rooms waiting for it. These folks

have sailed all the way from England, and they must be dog tired after the bumpy trip we just gave them.''

"What folks? You told me we was carrying nothing but m.a.b.'s.''

Agnes roared with laughter. "That's m.*o*.b.'s, cowboy. *Mail-order brides.*''

"Brides?'' Raider walked to the back of the wagon. "You're pulling my leg.''

"I got no reason to. Look for yourself.''

She opened the canvas flap at the rear of the wagon and stepped back. Raider peered in and saw six women between the ages of eighteen and thirty huddled together on the wagon's floor.

"I'll be a son of a bitch,'' he said, grinning. "No need to go out tonight. I'll just stay home and get to know these here lovely ladies.''

"You'll behave yourself or the Mormon will cut your balls off. Ain't you ever heard of those men out west who marry lots of girls at the same time?''

"You mean all these women are going to marry the same man?''

"Yup, Mr. Daniel Edmonds.''

"Well,'' said Raider, "they ain't married yet, are they?'' He surveyed the cargo again.

"Hell, no,'' said Agnes. "They ain't even met him!''

"Then they're free to do whatever they damn please.''

"Not exactly.''

"Why not? Who'll know?''

"You don't think I'm along just for my pretty face, do you?''

"That's for certain.''

"Read it yourself.'' She handed him a telegram. "I got my job to do, just like you got yours.''

Raider read the telegram aloud:

PLEASE SEND SIX BRIDES TO DANIEL EDMONDS IN SALT
LAKE CITY, UTAH, USA. STOP. APPEARANCE IS UNIM-
PORTANT, BUT MUST ALL BE VIRGINS. TO ENSURE THIS,
THEY MUST BE ACCOMPANIED ACROSS THE COUNTRY
BY A RESPONSIBLE FEMALE GUARDIAN WHO WILL AT-
TEST TO THEIR VIRTUE UPON ARRIVAL.

"I can't believe this," Raider said. "These girls are
beautiful."

"You'd be better off not looking. I can promise you
you'll just be wasting your time."

Raider looked directly at her. Her jaw was set, and her
hands rested on her massive hips.

"Yup," he said, "I reckon I would." But that was not
what he was thinking.

CHAPTER TWO

Raider walked into the dining room of the White Stag Hotel. It was an elegant restaurant with plush red velvet banquettes and crystal chandeliers. He felt out of place in his cowboy hat, jeans, leather jacket, and dusty, scuffed boots. He buttoned the jacket in an effort to look a little neater and then looked around until he saw where Agnes was seated with the six brides. He approached the table and cleared his throat conspicuously.

"For goodness sake," Agnes boomed. "I said you couldn't touch them, not that you couldn't go near them. Sit down." The brides looked at him and giggled. "Girls," said Agnes, "this here is Mr. Raider. He'll be riding with us to Salt Lake City. I'm afraid I ain't familiar with all your names yet, but I imagine Mr. Raider will learn them in due time."

Raider mumbled a greeting and sat at the table.

"I took the liberty of ordering your meal," Agnes told him. "I figure after all these years, I know a steak man when I see one."

Raider considered changing the order to spite her, but the fact was that he'd been thinking about a steak ever since Middletown.

"Now, girls," said Agnes, turning to the brides, "why don't you tell Mr. Raider and me how you like America."

"I think it's lovely," said one of the girls in a soft British accent. "It's even more striking than London."

"You come from London?" Agnes asked.

"No, ma'am, I come from the countryside, but I was in London when I was very small."

"Well," said Agnes, "where you're going is a lot more like the countryside than like this. We're still a long way from Utah."

"What's it like?" another girl asked.

Raider started to answer, but Agnes cut him off. "Mr. Raider would love to tell you about Salt Lake City, but he's never been there himself." The girls giggled, and Raider seethed inside. "Utah is really pretty," Agnes continued. "There are mountains and all the open space you could ever want. Best of all is the Great Salt Lake. It's so salty that you just lay in the water and float all day."

"What about Mr. Edmonds?" the first girl asked. "What is he like?"

"I can't tell you that," said Agnes, maintaining her maternal tone. "I've never met the gentleman myself, but I'm sure he's a fine man."

"I'd guess—" said Raider.

"Excuse me, Mr. Raider," Agnes said, interrupting, "would you be kind enough to fetch me a fork?"

Raider glared at her; she smiled. "I'd be happy to," he said through clenched teeth.

The girls' eyes followed him as he found a waitress, who brought the new fork. He noticed their interested looks but knew that any attempt at capitalizing on them would be blocked by Agnes. He returned to the table and finished his meal in silence. Then he put down his utensils and stood.

"I think I'll go out and see the city for a few hours, if

you don't mind,'' he said, knowing that Agnes would be angry but not caring. Besides, she was trying to appear sweet to the brides.

"Of course, Mr. Raider,'' Agnes said. "We'll see you later.''

As Raider turned to leave, one of the brides said, "Good evening.'' He stopped and turned around to see who'd spoken. She was about twenty years old and had long blond hair. She was dressed in a simple blue cotton dress buttoned to the neck and black shoes. Raider had noticed her during the meal, more for her quietness than for anything else, although she was very attractive.

"Good evening,'' he said.

He went outside and was surprised by how cool it had become. He walked the streets determined to find a saloon to his liking. He finally stopped in front of a small building with a sign that read "Robert McGuire's Tavern.'' He peered in the window and decided to try it.

He sensed that people were looking at him as he walked through the door and bellied up to the bar. It was a quiet place, and he heard a man say to his girl friend, "Take a look at the cowboy.'' But Raider was more interested in bourbon than in trouble. He ignored the comment and ordered his drink, gulped it down immediately, put the glass on the bar, and motioned for another. He picked up the refill and turned to survey the crowd. Several people who'd been staring at him looked away. He leaned his back on the bar and sipped the drink.

A young man in a full-cut white shirt, black pants, and suspenders entered the saloon and stood next to Raider. He ordered his drink, raised his glass to Raider, and said to the bartender, "Give this gentleman whatever he's drinking.''

Raider nodded his thanks, drank up, and put his glass on the bar. The man, who stood about six feet tall and had dirty blond hair and a wisp of a moustache, said, "It's easy enough to tell you don't come from New York." He wiped his hand on his pants leg and extended it to Raider. "Name's Russell Myers," he said.

"My name is Raider." They shook hands.

"So, Raider, where are you from?"

"Arkansas."

"Hmmm. I would have guessed a little farther west than that."

"I spend a lot of time out west. You might say I move around a bit."

"That explains it. What do you think of New York?"

"Lots of women and lots of whiskey, but I don't see much else."

"You play cards?"

"Poker?"

"If that's your preference."

"Where?"

Myers pointed to the back of the tavern, where a card game was in progress. Raider had a few extra dollars in his pocket and figured that poker would be more exciting than a night with Agnes.

"Sounds good to me," he said. "How do we get in?"

"Shouldn't be any trouble," said Myers. "Come with me."

They went to the back and within minutes were both in the game. Raider had a good run of luck and by nine o'clock had won almost six dollars.

"You're too hot for me," said one of the players. "I think I'll go to bed early."

Another man approached the table and asked, "Mind if I sit in, gentlemen?"

The players glanced up, mumbled their acceptance, and looked down at their cards. Raider studied the new man. He wore an expensive gray wool suit and had neatly combed black hair. A scar on the left side of his face extended from just below the eye to the side of his mouth. What Raider paid the most attention to, however, was the fact that he was armed. Raider had noticed that most of the men in New York didn't carry firearms, and now he was glad his own Remington 30-30 carbine was secure in his holster.

Before the new man sat down, a girl who was with him said, "Come on, honey, you can play cards any time. How many nights can you spend with me?"

"Leave me alone," the newcomer snapped.

"Oh, please," she said.

"I said leave me alone, you tramp."

He brought the back of his hand across her face, and she dropped to the floor. She started to cry. Raider was about to jump up and hit the man, but he realized that the other cardplayers were still staring at the table as though nothing had happened. He looked to Myers for an explanation, but Myers was as expressionless as the others. The girl got to her feet, wiped her eyes, and walked away.

"Gentlemen," said the new man, "shall we play?"

The dealer doled out the cards, and they resumed the game. Raider won the next hand, but the new man won the following one. After a dozen more hands, Raider realized that the man had won every other one and that the same cards seemed to appear in almost all of his winning hands. It was obvious that he was cheating, and he wasn't even making much of an effort to hide it. Raider knew that the other players were aware of it, too, but they seemed reluctant to say anything. Raider's judgment told him to toss in his cards and go back to the hotel. On the other hand, his personal code of honor told him to call the man out for what he was.

The man won the next hand with a full house, aces over fives.

"That's mighty strange," said Raider in a loud voice. "I got a pair of aces myself."

The whole bar hushed, and some people headed for the door. Myers looked at Raider and shook his head. Raider stared coldly into the cheater's eyes. The man laughed, and the other players uttered short, nervous giggles.

The cheater went to pick up the pot, but Raider grabbed his wrist.

"I don't think you ought to be taking my money," he said.

"You accusing me of cheating?" the man asked.

Raider stood and said, "I'm saying that there were five aces in that hand you won. You ain't getting my money, and I don't think you ought to take these boys' money, neither."

"Listen, cowboy, around here things are done my way. You don't hear any of these boys bitching, do you?"

"If your way includes taking my money, I'm afraid we're going to have to change the rules," Raider said as every eye in the tavern focused on the confrontation.

"Just what are you going to do to stop me?" the man asked.

Raider looked deep into the other man's eyes, a look honed by a long string of victories over lesser men.

"Okay, cowboy," said the man, "let's go outside."

The patrons of the bar cleared a path for them to walk through. Raider led the way. The other man took one step and then drew his pistol. Raider heard the hammer cock and instinctively fell to one side. A bullet that would have struck him in the small of his back whizzed by. He drew his Remington and fired three shots; each struck his opponent, making a neat vertical line on his chest.

As Raider stood and headed for the door, Russell Myers rushed up behind him and shouted, "Hold on a minute. You can't just leave."

Raider turned and faced him. "You saw what happened. The bastard tried to kill me. Anybody could see it was self-defense."

"That's not it, Raider. Don't you know who it was you killed?"

"Who?"

"Dick Jameson. He's one of the Dead Rabbits gang."

"I never heard of any Dead Rabbits gang. I don't know too much about gangs here in the East, but I seen enough of them other places to know they don't scare me. If that fellow is part of some gang, why was he running alone tonight?"

"Well, Yankee—he's the leader—and the boys are out west for a while."

"That so? What's he doing out west?"

"Don't really know. Folks say the boys are in Utah for a spell."

"Interesting," said Raider. "Maybe I'll get to meet Yankee and the boys, after all. Utah's where I'm heading."

Raider walked through the doors and returned to the White Stag. As he strode through the fancy lobby, a few heads turned. He didn't see Agnes or the girls; she must have them tied up tighter than a cinch on a bucking horse. He walked up the steps to his room and stood outside, fumbling for the key.

Suddenly a blond girl tapped him on the shoulder. It was the same girl who'd captured his attention at dinner.

"Hello there," Raider said.

"Hello." She smiled shyly.

"What's your name, little lady?"

"Molly."

"Well, Molly, what are you up to tonight?"

"Nothing."

"Why don't you come into my room? We can get to know each other."

She nodded thoughtfully and followed him inside. Molly, who was wearing a green flannel nightgown and whose long blond hair brushed her shoulders, sat on the bed, looked up at him, and smiled.

"Can I get you something?" he asked.

"No, thank you."

"You're pretty quiet."

"Uh huh."

"Tell me something, Molly. Why in tarnation would you want to marry a man who's going to have five other wives? It doesn't make sense to me, especially for a pretty girl like you."

She blushed and looked at the floor. "I was very poor in England," she said. "I came to this country so I wouldn't be as poor as me mum. I like to eat."

"So? Couldn't you find a man who wanted just you?"

"Can't you see?" she said softly. "I don't want to marry anybody I don't love, but at least with Daniel Edmonds I won't have to spend all my time with him. He'll have five other wives to keep him busy."

"Why don't you just drop out? Find another man and get hitched proper."

"Mr. Edmonds paid my way over from England. If I don't stay with him, he'll have me sent back."

"I think its the craziest thing I ever heard."

"Maybe," she said, "but it's better than starving."

"What will you do if you meet the right guy?" Raider asked, sitting on the bed next to her.

"That would be wonderful," she said. "I'd like nothing better than to meet a tall, handsome, strong American man. I'd bloody well give him anything he wanted. I'd belong to him." Raider lightly touched her knee. "But that will never happen," she said. "I belong to Daniel Edmonds, and I'll have to live with that fact for the rest of my life."

Raider removed his hand. "How old are you?" he asked.

"Eighteen."

"Where did you live in England?"

"I lived in a tiny farm town."

"You must have had lots of boy friends," he said.

"Goodness, no. There were very few boys in my town, and most of them married by the time they were fifteen. That's why I'm an old maid."

Raider laughed. "I'd hardly call you an old maid at eighteen."

"That's old for marrying where I come from."

Raider sensed that the girl was truly innocent, which was exactly what Daniel Edmonds was looking for. Although he would have enjoyed a pretty young woman before heading to Utah, he realized that he was wasting his time with her. At the same time, he was growing to like her and didn't want her to leave.

"It's getting late," she said, standing. "I think I'd best go back to my room."

"Okay," said Raider, grinning. "If I wasn't an old man, I'd marry you myself."

She giggled and left the room. Raider started to shut the door behind her, when Agnes walked up to him.

"I thought you were asleep," he said.

"I never sleep, especially with a horny cowboy around six virgins."

"Well, if they're all like Molly, you got the easiest job in the world."

"True. I knew you wouldn't have any luck with her. That's why I let her come in here."

"You knew she was in here?"

"Yup." Agnes sat in an upholstered chair. "I heard the whole thing. Happy to hear you play fair."

"That don't matter. I don't want you listening in on me."

"Sorry, sonny, but in my game you're the enemy." Raider slapped at the air and turned his back to her. "Relax," she said. "Want some hootch?" She held out a bottle of white rum.

"Don't mind if I do," Raider said, grabbing the bottle and drinking straight from it. He sat on the bed and asked, "Why do these girls want to do this?"

"Security."

"But they're so damn young and innocent."

"You only know Molly, Raider, and she's the only one I wasn't too late finding. Three of the others gave up jobs as London hookers to come here. The other two have been screwed more times than any six girls you know."

"What'll Edmonds say?"

"All I have to promise Edmonds is that these girls have been pure since I known them." She grinned. "He never wants them out of this lady's sight."

"Jesus Christ," Raider said before taking a long gulp from the bottle and passing it back to her.

"That was a rotten trick you played on me, Raider, running out like you did tonight. But I forgive you."

"I almost got myself killed doing it. Caught some fellow cheating at cards, and he tried to put a hole in me."

"And I suppose you put a hole in him."

"That's right. He belonged to a gang called the Dead Rabbits."

She chewed on her cheek. "Those are pretty rough boys. I've heard about them."

"I hear their leader's in Utah."

"Can't be. They're strictly out of New York. Gangs around here don't move around like boys out west. Why would he be in Utah?"

"I don't know the answer to that."

She took a swig from the rum bottle and looked at him. "So, how's a boy like you get involved with Allan Pinkerton?"

"I never met Allan Pinkerton. I just do what he pays me to do."

"What'll you do once we get to Utah?"

"Don't know. I'm supposed to meet Doc there. He'll have our orders." He laughed. "Hell, maybe we're supposed to bring back a Dead Rabbit, dead *or* alive."

CHAPTER THREE

Doc Weatherbee woke up when a ray of sunshine through the window of his room in King's Hotel caught him in the eye. He'd arrived in Salt Lake City the previous afternoon and had spent his first night exploring the town. It wasn't easy finding a live watering hole in the Mormon Mecca, but he'd managed, and the throbbing in his head reminded him that he'd stayed a lot longer than he should have.

He pulled the sheets over his head, closed his eyes for a minute, and then decided that he might as well get up and face the day. He dragged himself out of bed, pulled a bathrobe over his silk pajamas, and headed down the hall for a bath.

The hot water neutralized the hangover, and he returned to his room feeling slightly more human.

He laid out his clothes on the bed, stepped in front of a full-length mirror, and studied his face as though he'd never seen it before. His thick blond hair had been combed after he came out of the bath, and he patted a few stray strands until they were where he wanted them.

He drew back from the mirror and splashed a little cologne on his handsome face; then he drew close again and examined his blue eyes to make sure that his drinking spree hadn't left them too bloodshot. Satisfied with his appearance, he turned to the ensemble on the bed.

He picked up each item gingerly, as though they'd break if he squeezed too hard. He put on a white silk shirt, a brown cassimere vested suit, leather shoes, and five-button Melton overgaiters and topped it off with a pearl-gray derby, nestling it between his palms and making sure that it rested perfectly straight on his head.

He admired himself for a moment, removed a gold pocket watch from his vest pocket, checked it, and then took one last look in the mirror before going downstairs to the hotel dining room. He surveyed the crowd there. Off in one corner sat a well-dressed man in his late twenties. Doc approached him, looked around, and then sat at his table.

"Okay, Beckett," he said. "Let's hear it. What's so important in this town that you can't handle it?"

The young Pinkerton agent put his finger to his lips and then whispered, "It's big, real big, Doc, even for you."

"It's a town full of Mormons," Doc said. "I even had a hard time getting drunk last night. What the hell can they be pulling that you can't deal with?"

"First of all," said Beckett, "I'm off this case because Wagner said so, not because I ain't game. Second of all, does the name Jesse James ring a bell?"

"Jesse James?" Doc repeated as he removed a small diary from the inside pocket of his coat. "This isn't his neck of the woods. Is James here?"

"I ain't seen him, but word's out that he's on his way."

Doc laughed. "Beckett, do you have any idea how many times rumors go around saying Jesse James is coming to town? Hell, every town in the West thinks he's on his way to their neck of the woods."

"I know that, but every town in the West hasn't had outlaws pouring in for damn near a month."

"All right, Beckett, you have my interest. Tell me what you know."

"There's about a hundred known outlaws in Salt Lake City right now. Folks hardly ever see them, but the word is they're all staying on some big spread out of town. As far as I can tell, they haven't done anything wrong yet, and I don't know if they're planning to. It seems to me that if this many hired guns get together, they'll be looking to hit something a lot bigger than what's around here."

Doc carefully took notes about everything Beckett was telling him. He looked up and asked, "Who's here?"

"I can only vouch for the ones I've seen."

"Who?"

"A few Texas boys: Bill Longley, John Wesley Hardin, and Bill Raynor."

"Anyone else?"

He read from a list. "Rowdy Joe Lowe, Mysterious Dave Mather, the Clantons, the McClowerys, and Johnny Ringo."

"You heard these boys say that Jesse James is coming?"

"Yup, along with his brother Frank and Cole Younger."

"Well, I'll be. What would slingers like them want in this Mormon town?"

"That's what I've been wondering. They don't seem to do anything. It's more like they're here for some kind of party or convention."

"There hasn't been any trouble in town?"

"No, nothing big. There was a fight in a saloon last week. A couple of strangers started up with some locals."

"And?"

"The strangers beat the shit out of them, and that was that. They were a strange bunch, mostly Irishmen, and after the fight they drank and hung up a flag with a bloody rabbit on it."

"That can't be."

"Why do you say that? I saw it with my own eyes."

"The Dead Rabbit gang hasn't been out of New York in twenty years. What the hell would they be doing in Utah?"

"You know them?"

"I grew up in New York. The Dead Rabbits are some of the meanest sons of bitches I've ever seen. They make hard cases out west look like circuit preachers."

"Well, there was rumors going around that there were gangs here from Chicago and Philadelphia, too."

"It doesn't add up. There's nothing in the whole damn country worth splitting up a hundred ways, and there aren't too many things these boys couldn't take by themselves. It just doesn't make any sense."

"I already ruled out the banks, trains, and stagecoaches. They wouldn't be worth it. Problem is, I've ruled out everything else, too. There's just no reason for all these outlaws to be here at one time."

"What do you know about the Mormons?"

He shook his head. "I don't know a heck of a lot, but I doubt they're behind it. They're a religious bunch and a little crazy. A man can marry as many women as he can find, but he can't drink. Pretty dumb, huh?" He grinned.

"Some churches got an awful lot of money, Beckett. Maybe that's what they're after."

"I don't see it. If Jesse James wanted money from a church, he'd have it and wouldn't need a hundred men to help him."

Doc nodded his agreement.

"I just can't figure it out, and I reckon that's why Wagner called you in."

"To be honest, Beckett, I don't have any better ideas than you do."

Doc scribbled a few final notes in his journal and left the dining room without eating. He wanted to stroll around town and familiarize himself with his new surroundings in the daylight. He always felt uncomfortable if he thought that his adversary had an advantage over him, and he was determined to know Salt Lake City inside out.

He left the hotel and walked down the street. He'd seen all the stores and homes the day before, but this time he made note of small details, jotting down the names of shops in his journal: Gunderson's general store, McMahon's livery stable, Salt Lake saloon—nothing that would be of interest to so many outlaws from so many different places.

He went into the livery stable where he'd left his mule and wagon, approached the big black animal, and said, "Judith, baby, I missed you. How's my girl?"

He threw his arm around her neck and kissed her muzzle, patted her a few times, and then climbed into the back of the Studebaker wagon. He opened a trap door in the center of the floor and examined the contents of the compartment it concealed. There was a nickel-plated lever and trunnions for sending telegraph messages, a Premo Sr. camera, and a small arsenal of weapons. He pulled out a shoulder holster and strapped it on. Then he sifted through a few pistols until he found the .38 Diamondback he was looking for. Doc disliked carrying weapons but felt that under the circumstances he'd be foolish not to be prepared for anything. He thought about Raider. As much as he enjoyed goading Raider and as much as Raider's obstinacy could infuriate him, he wished that they were working together on this case. There were plenty of operatives who were better detectives than Raider, but Doc knew that when the going got tough, no one was more reliable than his rawhide sidekick.

He went to the front of the wagon and attached Judith's traces.

The stableman came over and asked, "You plan to be gone a long time, mister?"

"Could be," said Doc. "I've never been in these parts

before and thought I'd go take a look at the Great Salt Lake.''

"Well, you enjoy it, now.''

"Thank you, sir, I'm sure I will.''

He headed in the direction of the Salt Lake, continuing to study everything he saw along the way. It all appeared so ordinary to him: wooden houses and shops with wooden sidewalks running in front of them, a quiet place, not the sort of town where one would expect to find outlaws whooping it up.

He reached the Salt Lake and coaxed Judith to a stop. The lake was an impressive sight, a huge body of water with vast areas of open space around it. A few young boys floated on the salty water so effortlessly that Doc was tempted to take off his suit and try it himself. He resisted the urge and slowly walked alongside the water. Other people were scattered along the shoreline, and Doc took each of them in. One man seemed nervous when Doc's eyes met his. Doc sensed his discomfort and studied him more closely. He was a short, heavyset man with a goatee and a drooping moustache. His face was familiar to Doc, but Doc didn't know why. As they passed each other, the man looked straight at the ground, which prevented Doc from getting a closer look.

The man's face stayed with Doc as he continued walking, and he was so preoccupied with it that he hardly noticed other people, including a woman who looked directly at him as their paths crossed.

"Doc?'' she said. "Is it really you?''

"Huh?''

"Doc Weatherbee. I can't believe my eyes.''

"Emily?'' Doc studied the petite blond woman standing in front of him. She wore a long blue dress and bonnet and carried a closed parasol. "You look fantastic, Emily,'' he said. "I guess the easy life agrees with you.''

"Not exactly, Doc. Clint's dead."

"Dead? You must be kidding."

"He's been dead for five years now. Consumption."

"I'm sorry, Emily. I had no idea. All I knew was that he'd retired and wanted nothing to do ever again with Pinkerton."

"He was very fond of you, Doc. I think he missed you more than anyone."

"He was my first partner, Emily. He taught me everything I know. Guys getting shot up on the job is one thing. That we can deal with. But it's tough when a guy can make it through years of getting shot at and then keel over one day."

"Clint was so easygoing, at least until the end."

"What do you mean?"

"Something was bothering him real bad the last year. He never did tell me what it was. We moved from Oregon to Salt Lake City, and it just got worse. Then one day he got sick, and the next day he was dead."

"Sounds like he was trying to protect you."

"I thought so at first, but now I'm not so sure."

"Why?"

"You remember the way Clint was, Doc. He never got angry. He kept everything inside, and when he couldn't solve a case, it drove him crazy. He'd withdraw and become totally preoccupied. That's the way he was toward the end, too, about his life."

"That was just his nature, Emily. He took his work seriously, almost as seriously as he took loving you. His whole life centered on you. Sometimes, when we were on the road, he talked so much about you that I wanted to tell him to go home. That's probably how he felt about dying. What he couldn't deal with was being without you."

"I guess you're right. It's just that I'm still uncomfortable when I think about the whole thing." They stood silently for a minute before she said, "Doc Weatherbee, you are a sight for sore eyes. I never thought I'd see you again. I just can't tell you how good I feel."

"Me, too," Doc said.

"Why don't you come along to my place? We'll have lunch. I bet you haven't had a home-cooked meal in a long time."

"As a matter of fact, I haven't. I'd love it."

He helped Emily into the Studebaker wagon and climbed up next to her, picked up the reins, slapped Judith's rump, and sat back as the wagon inched along.

"Emily," he asked, "did you notice a short, heavy fellow with a moustache and beard along the lake?"

"No, I can't say that I did."

"He had a black goatee and one of those long moustaches. I know I've seen him before."

"It sounds like a lot of men around here. I'd have to see him to know for sure."

"Well, never mind. It's probably just my imagination."

Emily smiled. "You sound just like Clint."

"Like I said, he taught me everything I know."

She pointed down the road and said, "It's the white one over yonder."

Doc steered the wagon to a small house at the end of the road. He leaped to the ground and extended his hand. Emily took it as she carefully stepped down from the wagon. She opened the door to her house, and Doc stepped back to allow her to precede him. He followed and looked around.

"Nice place," he said.

"I thought it was the perfect place for us. I'm not sure if Clint ever really liked it."

"What made him leave Oregon?"

"I never liked Oregon, but Clint loved it. I had given up all hope of living anywhere else, when one day he comes down to breakfast and says, 'Babe, we're going to live in Salt Lake City.' He never did say why." She took Doc's hat and hung it in the hallway. They stopped at the entrance to a small room. "That was Clint's study," she said.

Doc walked in and looked at the desk. "That's his Pinkerton case journal," he said, pointing to a small, black book.

"He kept all of his Pinkerton things, Doc. That bag over there has his camera, telegraph equipment, everything."

Doc opened a canvas sack and removed a Diamondback pistol identical to his own.

"I remember the day you boys bought those guns in Tulsa," Emily said. "You were like a couple of little boys, always holding them and cleaning them. Clint hardly needed his. He left Pinkerton right after you bought them."

"It's funny," Doc said, his voice plaintive, "lately, I'd been thinking of trying to get an assignment up Oregon way so I could see you and Clint."

"I wish more than anything you could have seen him before he died. You were the only Pinkerton person he ever talked about. Anyway, I'm glad I got to see you. I can't tell you how much better it's made me feel."

Doc took her hand. "This all must have been very hard on you, Emily. I know how much you loved him."

"He's a hard man to forget." She was silent for a moment until Doc released her hand. Then she said brightly, "Just sit down, Doc. I'll get started on lunch."

He sat on a sofa in the study and looked around. There was a photo of Clint and Emily nailed to the wall. Doc examined it and remembered that he'd taken it himself in Denver when he got his first Premo Sr. camera. He was a novice at developing, and it was the only shot that came out, although he'd taken ten plates. Clint had ribbed him constantly about his photography, and it was that kind of good-natured kidding that had inspired Doc to improve many of his talents.

He looked through the door to the kitchen and watched Emily slice fresh vegetables on a wooden table. He thought back to when Clint had met Emily. Doc had been there. They were on vacation in Ohio after an assignment. Emily was much younger than Clint, only eighteen when they were married. Doc looked at her in the kitchen and figured that she was now at least thirty, although she'd changed very little. She was short but had long, slender legs and a full, womanly figure. He realized how beautiful she was as she gathered up the vegetables and walked across the kitchen, disappearing from his view.

His attention returned to the study. There were books on the desk along with a pen and a few pieces of yellowing paper. The room looked as though Emily hadn't touched it since Clint's death. Doc stared at Clint's Pinkerton journal and then picked it up.

"Doc," Emily shouted from the other room, "I have some coffee ready. Why don't you come sit in here until lunch is ready."

"All right," Doc said, replacing the journal without opening it. He went into the kitchen and sat at the table. "What smells so good?" he asked.

"Lamb stew left over from last night." She grinned. "Well, the night before, actually. I don't eat so much all by myself."

Doc laughed. "I can certainly help you there. I missed breakfast, and I'm starving."

"Wonderful. It'll be right out."

"Emily," said Doc softly, "I couldn't help noticing some of the things in Clint's study. It doesn't look like you've touched it."

"I haven't."

"Why?"

"It just seems too final, I guess. Those things are all I have left of him. If I threw them away, it would be like he was never here."

"I'm not saying you should throw them away, but maybe you could put them in a safe place."

"Maybe. Would you help me?"

"You can count on it."

She placed a large bowl of stew in front of him and took a smaller serving for herself. She sat down across from him and smiled.

"What about you, Doc?" she asked. "Still haven't found the right girl?"

"Can't say that I have."

"If I know you, you found too many of them and just can't decide."

"You flatter me, Emily."

"Do yourself a favor, Doc. Get away from Pinkerton before you're too old, find a nice girl, and live a proper life. But don't get married until you're ready to do that."

"You and Clint always seemed to manage okay when he was an operative."

"We did, but that was because we were in love. When you two were away on an assignment, I couldn't eat, I couldn't sleep, I couldn't do anything. I always wondered whether he'd come back alive. I even worried about you when I got tired of worrying about him. That's why I was so happy when he quit. The day he told me he was through, I felt like somebody had lifted a huge weight from my shoulders. I thought I'd never have to worry again about hearing he'd died. Then, next thing I know, he's dead. I was in shock."

"Clint was the best," Doc said, not knowing what else to say. "There were guys who could shoot better and guys who were tougher, but nobody was smarter or worked as hard. He was a born detective, Emily. He must have loved you an awful lot to give up Pinkerton."

Doc heard a horse ride up outside the kitchen window. He pulled back the curtain and saw a man, his back to the house, dismount a gray mare with a white face.

"My word," said Emily, "Clint certainly did teach you everything he knew. That was his most annoying habit. Every time a horse passed or a dog barked louder than usual, he had to check to see who it was."

Doc smiled but kept his eyes fixed on the man.

Emily peeked out the window. "It's just Mr. Schwartze," she said. "He's been living next door to us since we got here. He's a quiet man, doesn't have much to do with people."

Schwartze turned, and Doc recognized him as the man he'd seen near the lake. He saw Doc looking at him and quickly entered his house. As soon as Schwartze was inside, he pulled the curtains over all his windows.

"That's him," said Doc. "The man I saw down at the lake."

"What's wrong with that? I see Mr. Schwartze down at the lake often."

"I know his face. I'm not sure if he always had the moustache and beard, but I know I've seen him before."

"If you could take your mind off your Pinkerton training long enough to eat, you'd be a lot better off, Doc."

"Yeah," he said, taking a spoonful of stew in his mouth. "I suppose you're right."

CHAPTER FOUR

"Damn it to hell, Agnes, you hardly ever let me talk to anybody but Molly."

"Well, she's a sweet girl, Raider. I thought you two were hitting it off mighty fine."

"Sure we are, but that ain't the point. Why can't I get to know the other girls, too?"

"Because they ain't like Molly. They'd like to get to know you too well, if you catch my drift. Remember, cowboy, I've got myself an obligation to keep them away from the likes of you."

"What do you take me for?" Raider asked innocently, smiling like a little boy.

"Just what you are, a cowboy with a big cock."

Raider turned his attention to the horses pulling the wagon and gripped the reins a little tighter. It was late afternoon, and the sun-dried road threw up a lot of dust as the horses' hooves churned it.

Agnes coughed and said, "It sure is hot around here. Where the hell are we, anyway?"

"Ohio," said Raider, still sulking.

"Is that all? Christ, it seems like we've been on the road long enough to be in California by now."

"We'll be in Indian country soon enough," Raider grumbled. "Then we'll be moving faster."

"I passed through plenty of Indian territory in my time, Raider. They don't frighten me none."

"No, I don't suppose they would, Agnes."

"One thing that does frighten me is sunstroke. I think I'll climb in back with the girls and get a little shade. I'd appreciate you tying that nag of yours to the back of the wagon and taking over the driving."

Raider brought the big wagon to a halt, and Agnes climbed down from the springboard bench. She looked up and said, "You don't mind being alone for a spell, do you?"

"I'll manage."

"I'll send Molly up to sit with you."

"Whatever you say, Agnes."

A minute after Agnes disappeared, Molly climbed into the seat next to him. Raider chuckled aloud.

"What's so funny?" she asked.

"You. You're always so damned excited."

"Of course I'm excited, mate. I've never been to America before. This is all new to me."

Raider looked at her and smiled. Her long blond hair was pulled back into a ponytail, and her wide-open eyes lit up her entire face. She was tall and slender and had the awkward hint of a tomboy in her walk. She was basically a very shy person, but after two weeks with Raider, she'd begun to talk incessantly and even joke with him.

"Where are we?" she asked.

"Ohio."

"Is that anywhere near Salt Lake City?"

"Let's just say it's closer to New York."

"How long will it be until we get there?"

"That's hard to say. We're heading into Indian country."

"I don't remember seeing Indian country on the map Agnes showed us."

"It's not on the map," Raider said, laughing, "It's a place where Indians live."

"Like India?"

"No, not like India. A different kind of Indians—red Indians."

"Oh, I see, like in the Boston Tea Party."

"I don't follow."

"I learned it in school. The Boston Tea Party happened when the colonies had their revolution. A lot of them dressed up as red Indians and threw a boodle of tea into the bay."

"You're a little too smart for me, Molly. I ain't very good when it comes to school. From the sound of that story, I'm just as glad."

"I think you're very smart."

"Do you? Why, thank you."

Molly kept talking. The sun had begun to set by the time they reached a wide stream spanned by a wooden bridge. An old man with a gray beard stood in front of it.

"What does he want?" Molly asked.

"I reckon we'll find out in a minute," Raider said. He tugged on the reins, and the horses did a stutter step before stopping. "What's the problem?" Raider asked the old man.

"That's a mighty big wagon."

"Yeah, I suppose it is. What's it to you?"

"What's the wheel span?"

"I don't know."

Agnes poked her head out of the wagon and shouted, "It's seventy-five inches, cowboy. I thought I told you that."

"You heard the lady," said Raider. "Seventy-five inches."

"Just what I thought," the old man replied. "This here bridge is only six feet. You're three inches too big to cross."

"Can we drive it through the water?"

"Maybe, but it's deeper than it looks, and it has a muddy bottom. With a wagon this heavy, you'd be better off going to another bridge."

"Where?"

"About five miles south."

"That's too far. We wouldn't make it by dark."

"Suit yourself," the old man said before spitting and walking away.

Molly looked at Raider. "Let's try to make it through," she said. "I know you'll be able to do it."

"I don't know," Raider said, frowning. "This ain't the strongest wagon I ever seen."

Agnes came around to the front. "I hope you're not thinking about driving through," she said, "because if you are, we'll be in mud up to our eyes."

"Who died and made you boss?"

"Nobody, but if you try it, it'll have to be without me and the girls."

"You're always telling me what a pioneer you are, Agnes. What the hell are you afraid of?"

"I ain't afraid of nothing, but I learned a long time ago that when you're traveling a couple of thousand miles, an extra five miles ain't going to hurt you any."

"It'll be dark before we can make the other bridge," Raider said.

"That's right, cowboy. So we'll camp here."

"Camp here?"

"Why not? You start gathering up wood for a fire while me and the girls unload."

Raider went into a wooded area a hundred feet off the road and collected fallen branches and logs. He returned to the wagon and grabbed a felling axe.

"If we're going to do this, we might as well do it right," he said, returning to the woods.

"Okay, girls," Agnes shouted. "The cowboy'll be back with the wood in a bit, so let's get everything out of the wagon and make some dinner."

"What's for supper?" asked one of the girls.

"Beans."

"Just beans?"

"That's right, honey. All those hotel restaurants and Daniel Edmonds's pocketbook have got you spoiled."

A half hour later the fire was burning strongly. Raider made a stand to hold the pot, and Agnes dumped in the beans.

"I can't believe you expect us to eat that for supper," one of the girls said.

"You got to be kidding, little lady," Raider said. "My mouth's been watering for beans like this since we left Pennsylvania."

"They look good to me," Molly said, looking to Raider for approval.

"Good or not," said Agnes, "it's chow, and nobody's forcing anybody to eat it."

By the time they were finished eating, it was pitch dark. Agnes put on a pot of coffee, and they sat around the fire in a large circle.

"It's still mighty hot," said Raider. "I always thought it was supposed to be colder back east."

"I guess we got one of them heat waves," said Agnes.

"I like it," Molly said. "It reminds me of home."

"Where do you come from Molly?" another of the girls asked.

"Devon."

"Was it nice?"

"It was lovely, but my family hadn't a pound to its name. My father is Welsh. He was a lawman in Wales, but then he met me mum and tried his hand at farming. He wasn't very good at it. Both my parents got sick, and they thought it best that I come here instead of being a poor old maid in Devon."

"I'll bet you miss it," one of the girls said.

"I miss my folks, especially my dad. On nights like this, he used to take me out and we'd shoot at tin cans."

"Hold on," said Raider. "You shoot?"

"Sure," said Molly, smiling broadly. "My dad loved guns. Matter of fact, he once had a Winchester .44 like yours. He even had a Colt .45. Maybe that's why I like you so much. You remind me of Pop."

"That ain't a compliment," said Raider.

"Sorry," Molly said, giggling. "Make that a big brother."

"I still don't believe you can shoot a pistol."

"Things are different out in the countryside than in London. Give me a tin can."

Agnes handed Raider the empty bean cans. "I'd like to see this myself," she said.

Raider lined up five cans, and Molly said, "Me and my pop used to have a contest who could hit the most. He usually won."

"I'm pretty fair myself," said Raider.

"Wonderful," Molly said. "Me and you will have a contest."

"I'm not sure that's fair. You're just a young kid."

Molly put her hands on her hips, tightened her lips, and glared at him.

"Come on, bloke," shouted one of the girls, "you've been challenged."

"I think your pride is on the line, Raider," Agnes said.

Raider held out his pistol for Molly.

"Oh, no," she said. "You shoot first. I'm very superstitious."

Raider put the pistol back in his holster and stood thirty feet from the cans. He studied them for a minute, drew his gun, and squeezed off five quick shots. The first four cans flew in the air with holes in their centers, but the last can had only been grazed. It wobbled and stayed in place.

"That's four," Agnes announced.

"I think that ought to do it," said Raider, winking at Molly.

Molly didn't say anything as the cans were lined up again. She took the gun, stared at the new lineup, closed one eye, and held the weapon at arm's length. She fired, and the first can flew into the air. She adjusted her arm, paused, and then fired again. It was a direct hit. She then methodically drilled the third and fourth cans, and Raider felt the blood rushing to his face.

"Throw the last one," Molly said.

"What do you mean?" Raider asked.

"Throw it in the air."

"Just shoot it," Raider growled.

"Please throw it. It's more fun that way."

"I'll do it," said one of the other girls as she rushed to the remaining can. She looked back at Molly.

"Throw it," Molly said.

She threw the can high in the air. Molly fired, and her bullet split the can in half.

"There," she said, handing the .44 back to Raider. "I feel much better." The other girls hugged her.

"Next time you shoot first," Raider said sheepishly. He silently sat down by the fire.

"I knew it," said Molly, sitting next to him. "My father always sulked when I beat him, too."

Raider looked at her for a moment and then broke into a wide grin. "You're okay, kid," he said.

Agnes broke out a bottle of white rum from the wagon. "Don't you ever run out of that rotgut?" Raider asked.

"Hell no, cowboy," she said, "and I'd gladly trade you for another bottle." The girls laughed. "Besides, I haven't noticed you turning any of it down."

"No, and I won't tonight, either. I might just as well get drunk and forget what Molly did to me."

They passed the bottle around and finished it. Agnes produced another, and they killed that, too. Eventually, Agnes passed out on the ground. Molly went into the wagon and fell asleep.

Raider sat with the other girls. It was the first time he'd been alone with them since New York.

"You're pretty good with that gun," a buxom brunette named Ann who was sitting to Raider's left said.

"Had to be to keep alive. I'm still here."

"Can I see it?" she asked.

"Sure, but be careful. Don't hurt nobody."

She took the .44 from his holster and examined it. Then she replaced it in his holster and allowed her hand to slide over his crotch.

"It's getting late," he said as she continued to stroke him. She finally brought her fingers up to his belt and started undoing it.

"I think you ladies ought to get some sleep," he said. "We got another big day ahead of us tomorrow. Somebody help me put out the fire."

The girls stood. One of them turned and said, "Don't worry, Raider, Ann's good at putting out fires." They all laughed and disappeared into the wagon.

Raider turned to Ann and looked at her huge breasts. "Alone at last," he said as he took one in his hand. He pulled her closer and plunged his tongue into her mouth as she tried to unbutton his denims. Then they heard a groan from the other side of the smouldering fire. Agnes was coming to.

"Why don't you get some sleep, Agnes," Raider said. "That rum is murder." Ann hid behind him in the hope that Agnes wouldn't see her in the dark.

"Good idea, cowboy," Agnes said. "I could use a little shut-eye." She walked toward the wagon, swaying back and forth and at one point almost losing her balance and falling, which caused Ann to giggle. She reached the wagon, turned, and said, "You get some sleep, too, cowboy."

Raider thought that she was gone. He pulled Ann to him and started kissing her neck, when Agnes's voice bellowed, "Annie, get your hand out of the cowboy's pants or Mr. Edmonds might be inclined to send you back to London."

"Sheeet," Raider hissed.

"Sorry, cowboy, but that's my job," Agnes said, laughing.

CHAPTER FIVE

"Just a minute," Emily shouted before licking her fingers and wiping them off on a rag. She removed her apron, stopped in the hallway to look at herself in the mirror, patted her hair into place, took a deep breath, and opened the door. "Doc," she said, "you're fifteen minutes early."

"I never have been able to keep a beautiful woman waiting," he replied. "I guess it's just a bad habit."

"Not at all. Come on in."

"I've been saving this for a special occasion," he said, handing her a bottle of red wine. "I picked it up in New York a few years ago. I knew there'd come a time special enough to use it."

"Why, Doc, that's so sweet of you."

"It isn't every day you meet an old friend you didn't think you'd ever see again."

"No, I guess it isn't," she said, smiling. "I'll take the wine into the kitchen. Dinner will be ready in a little while."

Doc followed her into the kitchen and watched her remove a chicken from a reflector oven and put it on a large yellow plate. Before she could begin carving it, Doc said, "Allow me. You've worked hard all day to prepare this meal."

"Still a gentleman," she said.

"And you a beautiful lady."

He finished carving the meat and then sat at the table. She brought two glasses in from the other room and sat across from him. He opened the bottle, sniffed the cork, and poured. Emily looked at him and smiled.

"I still can't believe it's really you," she said.

"Oh, but it is," Doc said. "I can promise you that." He raised his glass and looked directly into her eyes. "To Emily Stover. Seeing you again makes all these lonely nights in new towns worthwhile. To your beauty, inside and out."

She looked down with a small smile and then sipped her wine. "It's delicious," she said. "I wish I'd made a more appropriate meal."

"Nonsense," Doc said. "This is one of the finest meals I've eaten since I left New York."

"That reminds me," Emily said. "You never did tell me what you were doing here in Salt Lake City."

"You don't believe that I traveled a thousand miles to see you?"

"Be serious."

"Actually, it could be a big case," he said.

"Who hired you?"

"I don't know."

"What do you mean you don't know?"

"Wagner wouldn't tell me."

"Don't tell me Wagner's still working for Pinkerton."

"He sure is, and he claims this fellow wants to remain anonymous. Apparently, he's afraid of stepping on some important toes."

"What does he want you to do?"

"Well, it looks like there's dozens of outlaws in Salt

Lake City right now, but nobody knows why they're here. They haven't caused any trouble yet.''

"Naturally, you're going to figure it all out.''

Doc raised his glass, winked, and said, "Naturally.''

They talked about each other's lives until they'd finished the entire bottle of wine. It was almost nine o'clock; the Utah night was coal black.

"That was absolutely the best wine I ever tasted in my whole life," Emily said. "I wish there were more of it.''

"I hadn't planned on telling you this," Doc said, "but the truth is, I've been saving two of those bottles for a special occasion. The other one is in my wagon.''

"You devil," she said, smiling coyly. "March yourself right out to that wagon and bring that other bottle in here. This is as special an occasion as you're likely to find.''

"Yes, ma'am," he said, rising to attention and saluting.

When he returned, she'd moved into the living room and was seated on the couch.

"I'm in here, Doc," she shouted.

"Oh, that's much better," he said. "Nice and comfortable.''

"Yes, Doc, that's what I hoped.''

He watched her out of the corner of his eye as he opened the second bottle. Finally, he faced her and noticed the faraway look in her eyes.

"Emily," he said.

She took the glass from him and sipped from it.

"Am I boring you?" Doc asked.

"Don't be silly," she said. "I was just thinking.''

"What about?''

"It's been so long since I've enjoyed anything like this. I haven't been able to sit down with a person I really care about since Clint died. It's been very difficult." She smiled broadly. "I feel like my life has started over.''

"Thank you. That's very flattering.''

"I spent all afternoon getting ready for this night."

"The supper was mighty good."

"I don't mean *that*, Doc. I mean *me*. I put on every dress I owned before I decided on this one. I combed my hair for hours. I practically wore out a path between my bedroom and the mirror."

"You do look beautiful, Emily. I like your dress. Blue is my favorite color."

"It's nice to have someone special to dress for."

"I understand how you'd miss that."

She looked deep into his eyes. "That's not all I miss, Doc." She continued the stare as she stood and walked to the middle of the room. She stopped, glanced over her shoulder, and then continued into the bedroom without saying a word.

Doc sat on the couch for a moment. Finally he stood, drained his glass, and followed her. She was seated on the edge of the bed. He sat next to her and kissed her neck softly. She emitted a soft moan as his tongue made gentle circles on her soft, white skin. He caressed her shoulders and back before unbuttoning her silk dress, and then he put both hands inside the garment and pulled it away from her. She moaned again, this time a little louder, and arched her body so that he could remove her chemise and bloomers. She stared straight at the wall, just as she'd done when he'd first kissed her.

He stood and hurriedly kicked off his shoes and frantically unbuttoned his suit, shirt, and vest. He looked at her and saw that faraway look in her eyes again. Her firm white breasts were perfectly shaped, and there wasn't an inch of excess weight around her waist. Her figure was as perfect naked as it appeared to have been when she was dressed, as perfect as the eighteen-year-old virgin Clint had married.

Doc pulled his silk shorts over a huge erection and knelt

beside her on the bed. She turned slowly and looked at him. Then she brought her hand behind her head and tugged on a blue ribbon. It came loose, and blond hair cascaded down over her shoulders.

"Please be gentle," she said. "It's been a very long time for me."

He gingerly cupped one of her breasts, and his other hand caressed her back, pulling her closer. They met, and their tongues probed each other's mouths. Emily started to breath heavily as Doc pushed her on her back and pressed against her. He kissed her eyelids while toying with an erect nipple; then he rubbed his thigh gently back and forth across her pubic patch. She lay still, her hands at her side, her head moving from side to side as she purred like a cat in heat.

Doc shifted his weight toward her chest. He kissed her neck and shoulders before drawing one of her breasts into his mouth. He gently encircled her nipple with his tongue and sucked, bringing as much of the soft flesh into his mouth as possible. He used his tongue to push her nipple against his teeth. She squirmed uncontrollably, and he switched to her other breast. After a few minutes of moaning and heavy breathing, she gasped, "I'm ready, Doc. I'm ready right now."

"Take it easy, baby," he said, his hand groping between her thighs.

She pressed them tightly together before spreading her legs and tossing back her head; her arms were stretched to their fullest length as if to invite Doc inside. He kneaded her soft, malleable thighs, and each time he drew closer to her mass of femininity, she moaned louder and her writhing intensified. Finally, he flicked her clitoris with his finger, and her hips went into spasm. He rubbed it.

She grabbed the ends of the bed and screamed, "Sweet Jesus, I'm coming."

As soon as her orgasm ebbed, she breathed deeply and said, "Let's do it, Doc. I really want to do it now."

Doc was more than ready. He moved on top of her, kissed her mouth, and felt her instinctively pull away as he slowly entered her. He continued to penetrate her hot, wet, velvet sheath until the entire length of his shaft was deep inside. She came immediately, digging her fingernails into his back and sobbing softly.

He thrust more rapidly, each move causing her nipples to brush against his chest. His climax was seconds away.

She sensed it and said, "No, not yet. I'm almost ready again."

Doc slowed down and grabbed her hair. She wrapped her legs around him and pulled him deeper into her. Their sexual release was simultaneous and prolonged; it was a full five minutes before they stopped twitching.

Doc rolled off her and lay on his back. He closed his eyes, and neither of them said a word for a long time. He was on the threshold of sleep, when his penis came to life again. He opened his eyes, looked down, and saw Emily moving toward his burgeoning erection with her lips. She kissed and licked him, and when he was completely erect, she took him in her mouth.

"Oh, yes," Doc said, "that's delightful."

Her fingers glided up and down his erect, pulsating, slippery cock as her tongue swirled over its tip. When his full desire had returned, she bobbed her head up and down, taking in a little more of him each time. Doc pushed her face away, grabbed her by the back of the thighs, and adjusted her body so that she straddled him. He held his penis and brushed her sexual lips with it.

"I just can't believe this," she gasped, laughing. "It's so good."

He moved his penis along the wet lips of her vagina until she couldn't hold out any longer. She sank down onto his erection, emitted a long sigh, and gyrated her hips until Doc finally released.

They lay in each other's arms and basked in the splendor of what had occurred. Emily spoke first.

"It was wonderful, Doc. It really made me think about a lot of things. It's easy to see why you always had so many girl friends."

"Thank you."

"I hadn't really thought about what I'm going to do when you leave. It will be lonelier than ever."

"You knew I wouldn't be staying."

"Yes, I did. I always did."

"You understand, don't you?"

"I really have no choice, do I?"

"I guess not."

"How long are you staying?"

"I don't know. However long it takes to break this case. It's really all up to Pinkerton."

"Yes, it's always that way. Do you know something, Doc?"

"What?"

"Fuck Pinkerton."

She put her head on his chest and brought her leg over his. He stroked her hair and she started to cry, her tears dripping onto his chest.

"Don't think about anything," he said. "Just try to sleep."

She rolled off him and turned away. He pressed against her back and cupped a breast in his hand.

"Good night, Doc," she said, "and thank you."

"Good night, Emily."

CHAPTER SIX

The rain pelted Raider's face and made it difficult for him to see the muddy road. All around him was thunder, lightning, and fierce winds. Steam poured off the backs of the Percherons pulling the wagon. He looked into an angry, dark sky. The storm had been going on for over an hour and showed no signs of lessening.

Agnes yelled from the back of the wagon, "We're not going to make it, cowboy. You'd better start looking for someplace to hole up. The only reason the wind ain't flipped us over yet is that the wheels are stuck in the goddamn mud."

They were still several miles outside of Lawrence, Kansas, and Raider knew that she was right. He said, "I don't reckon there's many white folks around here. We'll have to put in with Indians."

One of the girls looked at Agnes, her face a mask of fear.

"What's the matter, honey?" Agnes asked her.

"Is it safe for white women to stay with Indians? I've heard terrible stories."

"You don't have anything to worry about, dear. We'll

59

be on what's called an Indian reservation, land given to the
Indians by the government. They live peacefullike on it.
We won't meet any wild Indians till we get a little further
west.''

"Will they let us stay there?"

"I reckon we'll find out."

"I hope they give us something to eat," Molly said.
"I'm starving."

"Well, little lady," Agnes said, "if I was you, I'd
control myself. Indians eat mighty strange things, even on
reservations."

Raider guided the wagon to the entrance of the Delaware reservation, a tract of land forty miles long and five
miles wide. It sheltered the entire Delaware nation, one of
a half dozen tribes still in Kansas.

Most of the reservation was dotted with teepees, but
there were a few adobe buildings and log cabins. A white
man ran toward the wagon from one of the cabins and
waved for Raider to stop.

"Whoa," Raider said, pulling back on the reins.

"Good evening," the man said. He was out of breath.
"I'm Reverend Wilkes."

Raider tipped his hat. "Pleased to meet you, Reverend.
I'm hauling seven women in the back of my wagon, and
I'm hoping the Delawares will give us shelter from the
storm till morning."

"Of course, my son, I'm sure they will. Just ride straight
ahead."

"Much obliged."

Raider slapped the horses on the rump, and they trudged
through the mud a few hundred yards until two young boys
stepped in their path, one of whom pointed to a log cabin.
Raider climbed down from the wagon and went to the door
and knocked. A young Indian woman answered. She stepped
back.

Raider entered, took off his hat, which dripped water on the floor, and asked, "Do any of you speak English?"

"Of course," said an old Indian man with long gray hair, seated at the head of a table.

"I'm hauling seven women across country," Raider said. "We got sidetracked by this here bad weather, and we need a place to stay. It's not so much for me but for the ladies. They're not used to this weather."

"Bring them in," said the old man.

The women entered the cabin with hesitation and nervously glanced around, their bodies coiled against attack. None of them had ever seen an Indian before.

"Ladies," said the old man, "I am Mountain Cloud, chief of the Delawares. Come and sit at my table. No one leaves my village hungry."

Women and children moved to the floor to make room for the visitors. One young brave stood and left the cabin without saying a word. Mountain Cloud motioned for Raider to sit.

"Sir, you have not yet told me your own name," the chief said.

"Folks call me Raider, just plain Raider."

"This is my son, Brown Deer, and my daughter's man, James Lonborg."

Raider now realized that the man seated next to the chief was, indeed, a white man. Brown Deer sat motionless, his arms folded across his chest. Lonborg extended his hand.

"Pleased to meet you," he said.

"We have smoked buffalo meat and corn bread for you," the chief said.

Raider looked down at an unappetizing plate of brown, greasy meat.

Lonborg noticed Raider's dismayed expression and said, "It ain't so bad. It takes a bit of getting used to, but you'll learn to like it."

Raider turned to the women. "Eat up, girls," he said. "This may be all we get for a while."

Molly immediately picked up a dish and filled it with meat and a piece of bread. The other girls looked for her reaction. She ate the meat quickly without looking up. One by one the others, including Agnes and Raider, served themselves.

"See," Lonberg said, "I told you it weren't all that bad."

"No," Raider said, "it ain't bad at all."

Mountain Cloud went to a small wooden table near a window and picked up a pipe crafted from a tree branch. He placed green reeds in it and lighted them, inhaled, and then passed the pipe to his son. Brown Deer did likewise and passed it on to Lonborg, who repeated the ritual before giving it to Raider. Raider cradled the pipe in his hands. He didn't want to smoke it but knew that he'd offend the old man if he didn't. He inhaled and quickly blew out a long, thin line of white smoke. He was unsure of where to pass it next and looked at Lonborg, who motioned for him to hand it to a young Indian woman on the floor to his left. Eventually, everyone in the room, including the mail-order brides, had smoked from it.

"Supper is now over," Mountain Cloud announced. Most of the Indians left the room. "Mr. Raider," the chief said, "Mr. Lonborg will take you around the village and find you a place to sleep. I will make arrangements for your women."

Raider followed Lonborg outside, leaving Agnes and the brides alone with the chief and his son.

"So," Lonborg asked as soon as the door was shut behind them, "what the hell are you doing in Kansas with seven women?"

"They're mail-order brides. They're over from England, and I'm delivering them to Utah."

"They're going to live with them Mormons?"

"Yup."

"I'll take Indians any day."

Raider laughed. "How'd you wind up living on a government reservation? I thought these places were strictly for Indians."

"And their mates."

"You like it?"

"I needed to settle down. I come from Vermont, started traveling around, ended up living in seventeen states."

"You must have started awfully young, Mr. Lonborg. You don't look no older than twenty-five."

"Twenty-six. I headed out when I was fifteen and never got into the habit of overstaying my welcome."

"Until now?"

"Me and my wife live in one of these cabins. Believe it or not, I really do love that squaw. She's what keeps me here."

"Any kids?"

"We got ourselves two."

"I thought I saw a couple of half-breeds around."

"You sure did." Lonborg said, laughing. "You see half-breeds wherever you look, but most of them ain't mine."

"You mean other white men live here?"

"Six. The rest just visit now and then."

"I ain't sure I follow you."

"Well, you see, since the redskins been put on this reservation, marriage is what you might call relaxed. We get a lot of white men passing through, boys who come down from Lawrence to see our women."

"The husbands allow this?"

"Hell, they encourage it." He grinned.

"Why?"

"The Delawares are poor people. The government gives

them $165 a year for everybody on this reservation whether they're half-breeds or full-blooded.''

"How do you put up with something like that?"

"I don't. Me and my wife are different. Nobody messes with any of the women in the log cabins. They're the important females in the village.'' Lonborg led them to a log cabin. "This is my house,'' he said. "You can stay here tonight. Mountain Cloud will take care of the women.''

"I don't know about that. I'm supposed to be protecting those girls.''

"Don't worry, there isn't a more honest man, red or white, than Mountain Cloud. Anybody who'd hurt those girls will have to answer to him.''

They went inside the cabin, which consisted of two sparsely furnished rooms.

"Sit down,'' Lonborg said. "I'll get us some coffee.'' Raider sat at a plain plank table. Lonborg returned with two cups and a pot of coffee. As he was pouring, he asked Raider, "What's going on in the real world? I never get a chance to see newspapers no more.''

"You ain't missing much.''

"Come on, Raider, something must be happening.''

"We haven't been in Kansas long. I really don't know much about nothing.''

"You passed through Missouri?''

"Yup.''

"I lived in Missouri. What's going on back there?''

"The biggest topic of conversation back there was Jesse James.''

"Jesse's still doing it, eh?''

"You talk like you know him.''

"Not exactly, but I did see him once.''

"Really?''

"Yup. I got on this train in St. Louis, and after an hour or so the train stops, and who comes busting into the car but Jesse James himself, along with his brothers and the Youngers.''

''What did you do?''

''Wasn't much I could do. I sat there and watched. They was nice about it, went up and down the aisles taking anything they thought had value. I'd worked a month in St. Louis just to save up enough money for train fare, and I was dressed in mighty old clothes. Jesse himself comes up to me and says, 'You got any money?' I says, 'Honest I don't.' He shakes his head and walks away. In a minute they was all gone.''

''Did anybody go after him?''

''You know how folks are. They sat around telling stories, making it sound like they fearlessly escaped from Jesse James. They make a hero out of Jesse in Missouri and Kansas. Nobody would kill him even if they did catch him, except maybe a Pinkerton man. I hear Jesse's already killed a few of them.''

Raider suppressed a smile. ''I heard something about that myself,'' he said.

Lonborg answered a knock at the door. It was one of the Indian women who'd been at dinner. She had long black hair and an exceptional figure. Lonborg spoke to her in her own tongue, using hand gestures. He turned to Raider and said, ''She wants to sleep with you. Mountain Cloud said he'd take care of you, and this is his way. Do you approve? I know you're traveling with some beautiful women.''

''I approve.''

Lonborg said something to the woman, and she went straight to the cabin's other room.

''You can use my bedroom,'' Lonborg said to Raider. ''I know what it's like being on the road a long time.''

''That's mighty kind,'' Raider said.

He entered the bedroom, where the woman was taking off her deerskin dress. Raider undressed, and when they were both naked, they faced each other, saying nothing. The woman's face was serious. Raider forced a smile, but the woman did not respond. He pointed to a straw bed in the center of the room. She went to it, lay on her back, and spread her legs.

"You like to get the point, huh?" he mumbled as he knelt beside her.

She questioned what he'd said.

"Forget it," he said as his lips found hers.

CHAPTER SEVEN

It was nearly dawn when Raider awoke. The Indian woman was asleep on the edge of the bed. Raider got up, looked out the window in search of an outhouse, saw one, and then stumbled outside. He had to pass several teepees to get to it, and when he almost stepped out of his calfskin Middleton boot that was mired in mud, he glanced into one of them. Inside, Brown Deer was energetically screwing Ann, one of Raider's charges.

Raider laughed. She finally got away from Agnes, he thought to himself, wondering whether the chief had decided to keep Agnes warm for the night.

He stayed in the outhouse for five minutes. When he returned to bed, the Indian woman was gone. He lay down, closed his eyes, and fell asleep. An hour later, Lonborg came into the room.

"Wake up," he said. "If you want breakfast, you'd better get it now."

Raider rolled over.

"Let's go, Raider," Lonborg said. "Everybody else is up."

Raider sat on the edge of the bed with his head in his hands.

"My wife went to get some more corn bread," Lonborg said. "Come on out whenever you're ready."

Raider dressed. As he walked through the door, he stepped on a small necklace, a leather band with an unusual coral trinket on the end. He bent over and picked it up.

"What's that you got there?" Lonborg asked.

"I don't know." Raider held out the necklace. "I reckon that Indian girl lost it on her way out."

"Jesus Christ," Lonborg said, "you'd better put that back where you found it."

"Why? What's so important about it?"

"Nobody can touch that except her, not even me."

"Except who?"

"My wife."

"I don't get it."

"Just put it back."

Raider walked to the spot where he'd found it and placed it on the floor.

"Good," Lonborg said. "Those necklaces can be handled only by members of the chief's immediate family. They're supposed to have all sorts of power, including wisdom and protection from disease. But the natives believe they become worthless if touched by a commoner, especially a white man."

"I didn't mean nothing by it."

"I know, but you have to understand that the Indians have been humiliated. Their culture and way of life has been taken away from them, so they hang on to whatever they can."

"I won't tell her, I promise."

The door opened, and a young Indian woman walked in. She smiled and said, "You must be Raider."

"Yes, ma'am, I am."

Lonborg stood. "Raider," he said, "this here is my wife, Fall Leaf."

"It's a pleasure, ma'am."

"James has told me much about you. I am glad he was able to again have the company of a white man. I sometimes think it is difficult for him to live here."

"He's a fine man," said Raider.

"Yes," said Fall Leaf, "he is." She put a basket on the table and said, "Please, help yourself to corn bread."

As they ate, Fall Leaf's hand went to her neck. "My necklace," she said. "It's gone."

Although Lonborg had told him what to expect, Raider was surprised at her panic.

"Calm down a minute," Lonborg said. "I'm sure it's not lost. Let's look for it."

Fall Leaf glanced around the room, spotted the necklace where Raider had replaced it, and said, "Here it is." She picked it up, tied it around her neck, looked at Raider by way of explanation, and said, "It is very valuable."

After breakfast, Raider and Lonborg went outside to find Agnes and the brides. As they walked past Brown Deer's teepee, they heard a voice say, "No, leave me alone."

It sounded like Molly, but Raider couldn't be sure. Then the woman screamed, and Raider was certain that it was she. He burst through the tent's flap. Molly was backed against a wall, and Brown Deer had his hand on her shoulders.

"Make him leave me alone," Molly said to Raider.

"You heard her," Raider said. "She wants to be left alone."

"You enjoyed one of our women. It is only right that I do the same with one of yours."

"You already had one, you bastard, and you ain't going

to have this lady if she doesn't want to. Get out of here and leave her alone.''

Lonborg put his hand on Raider's shoulder.

"Raider, I'm scared," Molly said.

"I said get out," Raider shouted.

Brown Deer slowly left the teepee.

"He didn't do anything to you?" Raider asked.

"No, thanks to you."

"Get your things together. We'll be leaving here soon."

Raider and Lonborg went outside, where Fall Leaf was waiting.

"You got trouble," Lonborg said. "He thinks you insulted him."

Raider looked across the clearing. In the center of the teepees was Brown Deer. He held a knife in his hands.

"Shit," Raider said, "I don't need this."

Raider approached Brown Deer. A crowd gathered silently to watch as the two men circled each other cautiously. Every few seconds Brown Deer thrust the knife forward, feigning an attack. Then he charged. Raider dropped to the ground and caught the brave's foot between his legs. Brown Deer fell, and the combatants struggled for the knife. Brown Deer broke free and tried to ram the knife into Raider's throat, but Raider drove his right fist into the brave's chest, causing him to heave and to drop the knife.

Raider grabbed it and reversed positions with his injured opponent. He looked down at the helpless Indian, the knife poised over his eye.

Fall Leaf ran to them and dropped to her knees. "Please, Raider," she cried. "Please don't kill him. He is my brother."

Raider looked up into her eyes and then over his shoulder at Lonborg. The white man's face was expressionless. Raider got up and handed the knife to Fall Leaf. They both turned to see Mountain Cloud standing next to Lonborg.

"What has happened here?" the chief asked his daughter.

"Brown Deer and Raider fought over the honor of a woman. Raider spared my brother his life, which is more than Brown Deer was willing to do for him."

Mountain Cloud faced Raider. "Our customs are different," he said. "My son is a warrior, and so are you. You battled, and you were victorious. I thank you for showing the mercy your people so often lack, and I apologize for my son. You are welcome to stay."

"Well," Raider said, "I reckon we should be moving on."

"Wait," said Brown Deer, still lying in the mud. "My necklace is missing. The white man took my necklace."

The chief looked at Raider. "Is this true?"

"I had a hard enough time dodging his knife, Chief. I sure as hell didn't have time to steal anything."

"He's a liar," snapped Brown Deer.

Mountain Cloud looked at his son. "Could you have lost your necklace while struggling? Perhaps it is in the mud."

"It's not in the mud. I tell you, Father, he's a liar."

"My son has called you a liar," the chief said to Raider. "Our people put a great value on honesty. We must find the truth. If you have the necklace, you will be punished. If you do not, the punishment will be administered to my son."

"You mean you want to search me?"

"That is the only way."

Raider looked to Lonborg, who nodded. "I suppose I don't have much choice," Raider said.

The chief motioned to his son, who got off the ground and approached Raider. He ran his hands through Raider's pockets and found nothing. He stepped back and hung his head.

"I am deeply sorry," said the chief. "I hope you will accept my apologies."

"I do, Chief," Raider said, staring at Brown Deer. "I certainly do."

Agnes pulled the wagon into the clearing, and Raider and the girls loaded up. They said good-bye to the Lonborgs and to the chief and then left the reservation.

By the time they reached Lawrence, Raider was driving and Ann was seated next to him.

"Did that Indian scare you?" she asked.

"Nope. I seen plenty of men tougher than him, with or without knives."

"He wasn't much in bed, either. I bet you'd beat him there, too."

"There ain't much sense talking about that."

"I was hoping you'd kill him. Why'd you let him go after what he did to you?"

"I don't know. I didn't see any reason to kill him."

"Well, I took care of him, anyway."

"What are you talking about?"

She pulled a jade necklace from her purse identical to the one Raider had found on the floor of Lonborg's house. "I took it from him while he was busy," she said, giggling.

"God almighty," said Raider, "you could have gotten us all killed."

"Well, I didn't, did I?"

"No, you didn't, but from now on you watch yourself, hear? Folks out here don't need much of a reason to kill anybody, including pretty young girls. You hear what I'm saying?"

Another giggle. "I hear you, Raider, I hear you."

CHAPTER EIGHT

"I hope you don't mind having scrambled eggs again," Emily said as she served Doc his breakfast. "I have so much bacon and eggs around here, you should be thankful I haven't been giving it to you for lunch and dinner, too."

"I love scrambled eggs," Doc said. "I also love bacon, but most of all I love having breakfast with you."

She finished serving the meal and sat down at the table. She'd just picked up her fork, when somebody knocked on the door. "Just my luck," she said. "It'll probably be stone cold when I get back."

"Let me," said Doc.

"Just eat your breakfast," she said, standing. "I'll be right back."

She returned to the dining room. "It's for you, Doc."

He shoveled another forkful of food into his mouth and wiped his chin with a napkin. He walked into the foyer, where the desk clerk from King's Hotel stood.

"What can I do for you?" Doc asked.

"I'm sorry to bother you, sir, but you left word that you would be here, and it's really an urgent matter."

"That's quite all right. What seems to be the trouble?"

"A wagon train's been hit by Indians. We got a lot of hurt people down at the hotel, and Doc Hastings is going to need a hand."

"I understand. You go ahead, and I'll be along as soon as I get my things."

"Thank you, sir."

The clerk left, and Doc turned to Emily. "Indians hitting a wagon train so close to town?"

"It happens pretty regularly around here." She sighed.

"Which tribe?"

"I don't know. I never heard anybody mention a specific tribe."

"Well, I better get over there."

"What are you talking about? You know as well as I do that you don't know anything about medicine. You've been using that story since the day I met you."

"Yeah, but I've learned a few things since then. Besides, I don't want to blow my cover."

"Well, do me a favor and don't operate on anybody."

"I promise."

He found a dozen wounded people lying on sofas and chairs in the hotel lobby, walked up to one of them, and asked, "Where is the doctor?"

"*Je ne parle pas anglais,*" said the man.

Doc walked around the lobby until the clerk came down the stairs carrying towels. "Oh, Dr. Weatherbee, thank you for coming," he said. "Doc Hastings will be down shortly."

"All right."

A moment later, a tall, dark-haired man in a black suit descended the stairs. "Keep these towels coming," he told the clerk.

"Dr. Hastings," said the clerk, "this is Dr. Weatherbee, the one I told you about."

"Oh, yes," said Hastings. "It's a pleasure to make

your acquaintance, Weatherbee.'' The two men shook hands.
''What is your specialty? Are you a surgeon?''

''No,'' said Doc, looking away for a moment. ''I specialize in homeopathic medicine.''

''I see,'' said Hastings. ''You're trying to tell me you're a medicine man.''

''Right.''

''Well, I don't suppose you have any magic elixir to help gunshot wounds, do you?''

''I'm afraid I don't.''

He sighed. ''Well, at least you can assist me while I make my rounds here.''

''I'd be happy to.''

Hastings knelt next to a woman who had a large bullet wound in her right shoulder. Doc passed him the alcohol, and Hastings began to clean the gaping hole.

''It's not too bad,'' Hastings said in a reassuring voice.

The woman, who spoke only French, looked at him and managed a faint smile.

''If you ask me,'' said Doc, ''they ought to hang every bastard caught selling rifles to Indians.''

''I agree,'' Hastings said. ''Only these folks have been shot with pistols.''

''All of them?''

''The ones I've seen.''

''That's odd,'' Doc said. ''Normally, Indians wouldn't be using pistols.''

''I never really thought about it,'' Hastings said. ''Fact is, this isn't the first time.''

''Do you know what tribe is doing it?'' Doc asked.

''Could be any number of them. Without seeing their arrow markings, it's hard to tell.''

''Do any of these folks speak English?''

''That fellow over in the corner. His name is Jack.''

Doc approached a middle-aged man on a sofa in the

corner of the lobby. A blood-soaked tourniquet was wrapped around his right calf.

"Are you Jack?" Doc asked.

"Jacques," the man replied, correcting him.

"I'm Dr. Weatherbee, Jacques. Are you all right?"

"I was lucky. Most of my friends are hurt worse than I. I was shot only in the leg."

"Are you with your family?"

"No, thank God. I was on my way to join them."

"Where?"

"The Northwest Territory. They have been there for several years. I am paid to guide wagon trains of my countrymen to Washington and Oregon."

"And you were attacked by Indians?"

"That is what happened."

"Do you know which tribe it was?"

"I do not."

"What type of weapons did they use?"

"Guns."

"Rifles?"

"A few, but most were firing pistols. I had little chance to notice details."

Doc paused to write in his case journal and then said, "You say you're paid to lead these wagon trains? You've done it before?"

"Several times."

"Has this ever happened before?"

"No."

"You've never found this area to be dangerous?"

"I was taking a new route on this trip. I thought it might save time. That is why I feel responsible for what has happened."

Doc jotted a few more notes in his journal.

"Doctor," Jacques said, "I would be happy to tell you everything I know, but later. I don't mean to be uncooperative, but isn't there something you can do for my friends instead of questioning me?''

"Certainly," Doc said. "Thank you for your time." He returned to where Hastings had just finished dressing the woman's wound. "It doesn't look too bad," Doc said. "At least nobody got killed."

"They killed a little girl," Hastings said, "but that isn't the worst part."

"Oh?"

"These people didn't even resist. They left their wagons and ran for the hills. The red devils shot them, anyway, like they were game."

They returned their attention to the patients and eventually finished treating them. It was early afternoon, and they decided to have lunch together in the hotel dining room. They sat by a window which looked out over an alley and the wall of a bank.

"Nice view," Doc said sarcastically.

Hastings managed a smile. "Well, the food is good, which is more than I can say for most places in Salt Lake City."

"How long have you been here?"

"About a dozen years. I married a local girl."

A heavyset blond waitress approached the table, coughed, and asked, "Would you gentlemen like to see menus?"

Doc perused his menu and remarked, "To tell you the truth, Doctor, the first thing I need after a morning like that is a good stiff belt."

Hastings emitted a small laugh. "Well, you've certainly come to the wrong place."

"How's that?"

"This is Mormon country. Surely you've noticed that by now."

"I know the Mormons aren't supposed to drink, but I managed to do all right in a saloon last night."

"You were lucky. There aren't many of them around, and they're closed more often than they're open. At any rate, you can be sure they don't serve alcohol in here. How about a sarsaparilla?"

"Very funny."

They ordered their meals, and Doc nursed a glass of water as he questioned Hastings. "You say the Indians have hit a bunch of wagon trains?"

"Ten or twelve this year."

"Always immigrants?"

"Yes."

"How about the locals? Do they have trouble with the Indians?"

"Nothing to speak of."

"Where do you suppose these Indians are getting the guns? It would have to be somebody around here."

"I suppose, but that doesn't help us any. Mormons have their share of swine like every other group."

"It shouldn't be hard to find a man who's selling pistols by the dozen."

"Maybe so, but why are you getting so worked up? You're only passing through."

"Yes, you're right," Doc said.

They ate in silence for a few minutes before Doc asked his next question. "What did you do with the spent shells you pulled from those folks?"

"They're still in my pocket. Some of the kids like them for souvenirs."

"I'd like a few souvenirs myself," Doc said. "Do you think you might be able to give me a couple of them?"

"Sure." Hastings reached into his suit pocket. "Take them all if you want."

"Much obliged," Doc said. He put the shells in his own pocket and was about to resume eating, when shouting in the lobby caused both men to look up.

"Come on, Frenchy," yelled a man with a thick Irish brogue, "you don't want to be getting blood all over the same carpet me and my friends'll be walking on. Why don't you show some manners and move on."

There was much laughter as a group of men appeared in the dining room's entrance. In front was a tall, thickly muscled man with red hair. The collar of his white shirt, coupled with his muscular build, made him look as though he didn't have a neck.

"Who's that fellow with the red hair?" Doc asked Hastings, conscious of having seen him someplace before.

"Beats me. It's the first time I've seen him."

The big redheaded man moved across the floor of the dining room toward Doc and Hastings; his cohorts were clustered together several feet behind him. They sat at a table fifteen feet from the one Doc and Hastings occupied.

"You know," said the redhead loudly when they were all seated, "I'm beginning to like this town more and more. You don't have to work as hard for your money."

Doc stared at him. His skin was covered with red blotches, and angry veins lined his nose. "Yankee Sullivan," Doc said under his breath. "I see it, but I don't believe it."

"What are you saying?" Hastings asked after washing down the last of his food with a glass of water.

"That Irish fellow," Doc whispered. "His name is Yankee Sullivan. I don't know what he's doing in Utah, but it can't be good. He's strictly bad news."

"How do you know him?"

"I haven't seen him in fifteen years. Fact is, I only saw him once, I was just a teenager when his gang, the Dead Rabbits, came into my neighborhood. They beat us up and took everything we had. They were mean sons of bitches, but none of them as mean as Sullivan, I hear he's the leader of the gang now."

"I don't follow you. I thought you were from back east."

"I am, New York. That's why I can't believe the Dead Rabbits are out here in Utah."

Doc and Hastings finished their meals and said good-bye. Doc headed back to Emily's. He was several hundred feet away from her house when he saw two men on horseback. He recognized one as John Schwartze, Emily's next-door neighbor. The men stopped in front of Schwartze's house. Schwartze wore a square blocked cap with no brim. The other man was short and stocky and had auburn hair. They talked for a few moments in front of Schwartze's door, and the stranger did a lot of laughing, but Schwartze's face never changed expression.

Finally, Schwartze opened the door and went inside. The other man mounted his horse and rode toward Doc. As he passed, Doc studied him. He wore a fine wool suit and had the same blotchy, fair skin as many of the men at Sullivan's table in the hotel. Doc watched the man ride into town, dismount, and head into the King's Hotel. Well, Doc thought to himself, this case is getting more interesting by the minute.

He walked up to Emily's house, knocked lightly, and then walked in without waiting for an answer. "Emily," he called.

"In a minute."

He nervously paced the living room and tried to piece together what information he had. He didn't hear her walk into the room behind him.

"I didn't have a chance to make lunch," she said.

"What?" He spun around.

"I said I didn't make lunch. I didn't know when you'd be coming back."

"Oh, that's all right. I had lunch with Doc Hastings."

"That's nice. What happened to the wagon train?"

"Indians shot it up."

"Was anyone killed?"

"A little girl. They gunned her down."

"How awful. What motivates people to do such terrible things?"

"I don't know about the Indians, Emily, but we've done some pretty bad things to them ourselves. Hastings tells me these folks were shot with pistols. That means somebody around here has been selling them to the Indians. He's the one who ought to be killed."

"Who would do such a thing?"

"Hold on, Emily. It just hit me." He slapped his head and plopped in a chair.

"What hit you?"

"It all makes too much sense, damn it. Every outlaw in the country has been pouring into Utah, and all of a sudden, every Indian who wants a pistol gets one."

"I'm not sure I understand."

"Can't you see? Selling guns is a profitable business, especially selling them to Indians. There's a fortune to be made, and there has to be someone around here who's setting it all up, masterminding it. If I'm right, and if it isn't stopped, every Indian in the country, on or off a reservation, will have whatever gun he wants, and that means nothing but bloodshed."

"My goodness, what are you going to do?"

"Find out who's at the center."

"How?"

"I have a pretty good idea already. I just ran into an old New York gang in the hotel called the Dead Rabbits. I saw them hurt a lot of people when I was a kid. They're big-time, and they wouldn't be here if it wasn't worth their while. I have a hunch they could be behind it. I also think your neighbor, Schwartze, might have his hand in it."

"Mr. Schwartze? That's ridiculous. He's never made a bit of trouble in all the time I've known him."

"Well, I just saw him talking to somebody I think belongs to the Dead Rabbits. Tell me, what does he do for a living?"

"Nothing. Folks say he used to be a prospector. He probably made enough money doing that to support himself."

"Maybe. Or maybe he's prospecting guns to the Indians."

"What are you going to do?"

"Find out where all these outlaws are holed up and see for myself. I'll bring along the camera and take what pictures I can. I don't mind telling you, Emily, I'm not exactly eager to walk into the middle of this."

"Is that Doc Weatherbee I hear talking? I remember a time when you'd walk into a room full of gunslingers with nothing but your bare hands."

He laughed. "I guess I'm older and smarter."

"I'm glad to hear that. Maybe I won't worry as much."

"To tell you the truth, Em, I wish my partner were along with me on this one."

"What's he like?"

"His name is Raider, and he has got to be the biggest, dumbest country boy this side of the Mississippi. But somehow he makes it all work to his advantage. I can spend hours explaining to him how Pinkerton wants something done, and then he ignores me and does the job his own way. He's big, mean, strong, and savvy, and there isn't anything he can't do."

"Sounds like quite a man."

"That he is, crazy but loyal and fearless. When the going gets tough, there's nobody like Raider, and I have a gut feeling the going is about to get tougher than any of us would like to see."

CHAPTER NINE

"What do you mean, 'the bishop's,' " Doc asked Emily. They were in bed, naked and spent after an afternoon of lovemaking.

"You heard me," she said. "The only place big enough to house all the people you're talking about is the bishop's estate. It's an unofficial headquarters for the church around here."

"Emily, I'm not talking about a bunch of Mormon altar boys. These men are killers and bank robbers."

"You asked me a question, Doc, and I answered it. The only estate I know of that could hold a hundred people is Bishop Lee's."

"Jesus Christ, I don't believe this. How do I talk to a bishop about this?"

"I met Bishop Lee a few times. Clint took a sudden interest in the religion, and Bishop Lee came over for tea once or twice. He seemed like a very nice man."

"Clint thought of becoming a Mormon?"

"I don't know how serious he was. Nothing ever came of it."

"Thank goodness for that. I think Clint drank a little too much for a Mormon's taste."

"I suppose he did." Her laugh was reflective, appreciative.

Doc got up and dressed. "I think I'll pay the bishop a visit."

"Come and see me as soon as you get back."

"I will." He opened the front door, and bright sunlight filled the small house. "Damn, I almost forgot," he said, going to the living room and picking up a cloth satchel from the sofa. "Where's the post office, Emily?"

"In Gunderson's."

"Thanks. I'll see you later."

Doc stepped outside into the blazing heat. Before claiming his wagon from the livery stable, he went to the general store to post his package. A cowbell tied to the door jingled as he entered and made his way down a narrow aisle between two rows of burlap flour sacks.

"Hello," came a female voice from the rear of the store.

"Good day," Doc said, straining to see above the sacks. "You certainly have enough flour."

He came to the end of the aisle and saw a woman of average height. She had extremely fine features and a full head of blond hair rapidly giving way to gray.

"We are Mormons," she said. "Our diet is very important to us, and we believe in lots of grains and vegetables."

"Well, I generally prefer a nice, juicy steak."

"Too much meat, like too much of anything, will lead to health trouble, Mr. . . . ."

"Weatherbee, Dr. Weatherbee."

"Oh, listen to me," the woman said, laughing. "Here I am telling a doctor about good health."

"That's quite all right. Your advice seems to have worked well for you."

"Yes, it has. I feel as sprightly after eight children as I did when I was a young girl. What can I do for you, Dr. Weatherbee?"

"I was told I would be able to post a package here."

"Certainly."

He reached into his jacket pocket and removed the satchel, opened it, peered inside at the assortment of bullets Hastings had given him, and then retied it. "I'd like to send this," he said, putting it down on the counter. "Would you be able to package it as well?"

"It would be my pleasure." She took a fountain pen and a bottle of ink from beneath the counter and flipped a page in her ledger.

Doc handed her a card. "Please send it to Mr. Wagner at this address in Chicago."

She took the satchel and tossed it on a small scale. "That will be three cents postage," she said.

"How much for a box?"

"That's on Mr. Gunderson and me."

"That's very kind of you. Much obliged."

He walked across the street to the stable and headed straight for his mule. "There's my girl," he said, hugging Judith's neck. "I missed you, baby."

A stableboy came over, and Doc handed him his ticket.

"How long will you be gone?" the boy asked.

"Don't know," Doc said. "I hope to be back around suppertime."

He headed toward the lake and soon saw the bishop's house in the distance. He continued along a path on the lake shore and in twenty minutes had reached the grounds of the bishop's estate. The greenery was lush, unlike most of Utah's arid, desert land. A huge white house surrounded by a dozen smaller buildings stood in the center. Doc judged the spread to be at least a hundred acres.

He navigated Judith past several small groups of people, hoping that he might recognize some, but none were familiar. He tugged on the reins, and Judith coasted to a stop directly in front of the main house's massive wooden doors. He approached them and slapped a brass knocker against the wood. A few seconds later the door opened and a young, fair-haired man faced him.

"I don't suppose you're the bishop," Doc said.

"I'm afraid not. I'm an Aaronic priest. My name is Father Moody."

Doc extended his hand, but the man ignored it. Doc tried again, and this time the young priest took it and said, "Forgive me."

"That's quite all right. Would you tell me where I might find the bishop?"

"You want to see Bishop Lee?"

"Yes."

"Whom should I say is calling?"

"My name is Dr. Weatherbee."

The young priest turned and walked slowly down the corridor, turning every few steps to check on Doc, who'd stepped into a large foyer and closed the doors behind him. The house was modestly furnished, in contrast to its grandiose exterior. There were a few religious items and samplers on the wall but little of the expensive furnishings and decor Doc had anticipated.

Father Moody returned and asked Doc to follow him. They retraced Moody's steps down the long hallway until taking a left and stopping in front of a set of doors. Moody opened them and stepped back to allow Doc to enter.

Doc stepped inside and saw a man standing behind a large, mahogany desk. This room was lavishly furnished, and many massive paintings of Western scenes hung on the wall.

"How do you do," the man said. "I'm Bishop Lee."

"Doc Weatherbee," said Doc, extending his hand.

As Lee clasped it, Doc studied the bishop's rugged features and took note of his firm grip. Lee stood better than six feet tall and had very broad shoulders. His hair was dirty blond with graying temples, and he was dressed in a black wool suit. All in all, he was not what Doc expected a bishop to look like.

"What can I do for you, Brother Weatherbee?" Lee asked.

"It's not 'Brother,' I'm afraid. I'm not a Mormon."

"That's all right," Lee said. "We're all brothers in life."

"Yes," Doc said, "I suppose we are. In fact, that's why I'm here to see you."

"Go on."

"I'm from New York. I'm on my way home from a medical symposium in California and stopped to visit an old friend, Emily Stover, here in Salt Lake City."

"Is that so?"

"Mrs. Stover told me that her late husband, Clint, had expressed interest in becoming a Mormon before his untimely death."

Lee turned his back to Doc and walked silently across the floor. He sat on a sofa, put clasped hands to his mouth, and then said, "That's true. Clint Stover did show an inclination toward our way of life before he died."

"Well," Doc continued, "I've always had a great deal of respect and love for Clint, and I've been thinking that this might be the proper way of life for me, too."

"May I ask how you know Clint Stover, Doctor?"

"My oldest brother and Clint were educated together back east. Clint was more like a brother to me than my own blood relation was."

"May I ask what religion you've been practicing until now."

"Truth is, I've never put much stock in religion. I guess seeing what happened to Clint has made me realize how important living the good life is. I keep thinking that it could have been me instead of him."

"How true, Doctor, and it's a good start."

"Folks around here seem so nice and friendly, Bishop. Your religion seems more . . . well, more relaxed than many I've seen. Even you reflect it. I expected to see a little old man in robes."

Lee laughed. "Sorry to disappoint you," he said. "Truth is, I'm more than a bishop. I've been a government Indian agent for close to twenty years now."

"Is that a fact?"

"Yes, it is, and I'm proud of it. I believe all people should harmonize in life, and that includes white men and Indians."

"That's admirable."

"So, Doctor, what would you like to know about our religion?"

"To be honest, sir, I've spent a lot of time traveling across the country as a single man. I've been known to drink a bit, and I can't say that I've been chaste."

"Doctor, what you've done up until now doesn't concern us. We're only interested in making your life better once you've seen the light."

A young woman entered the room and said, "Excuse me, Bishop Lee, can I take away your plate now?"

"Yes, of course," he said. He looked at Doc and said, "I was just finishing my lunch when you arrived. I've been very busy and haven't been able to keep to a regular schedule."

The woman turned from the table and stumbled. Doc grabbed her by the elbow and helped her regain her balance.

"Are you all right?" he asked.

"Certainly," she said. "Thank you."

Doc bent over, picked up the remains of a T-bone steak that had fallen, and replaced it on the plate.

"Thank you again," said the woman as she left.

"As I was saying," Bishop Lee continued, "we take a slightly different approach to honoring the father than you're probably used to. We don't believe in what some preachers call hellfire and brimstone. We prefer to think each man's reward comes in a degree commensurate to his way of life. All men can be saved, not just a chosen few."

"That's very generous of you."

"It's God himself who's generous. I'm just his agent."

"I have to confess, sir, that I'm troubled by something I've heard around town."

"Oh? What's that?"

"I've heard it said that your estate is being used to harbor criminals. This doesn't seem possible to me, but I'd be remiss if I didn't try to establish the truth for myself."

"There *are* many outlaws here right now, Doctor."

"I'm not sure I understand. You seem to be a law-abiding man."

The bishop laughed. "I am, Doctor, I assure you of that, but you must look at things from the philosophy I just explained to you."

"I don't follow."

"Who needs to be shown the right way more than an outlaw? I offer them a comfortable place to stay, and I am able to persuade them to the ways of the Lord. It's my mission in the world, one I take very seriously."

"But some of these men are murderers."

"I'm not here to judge, Brother Weatherbee. I'm sure many amongst us would find your lack of temperance or chastity intolerable, but it is our way to open our arms to everyone, including someone like you, or them."

"Yes, I understand. I do worry about one other thing, however."

"What is that?"

"The fact that so many gunslingers are together in one place could spell trouble for the honest and innocent people of your community."

"I must confess I almost let that persuade me, but I polled my congregation, and it agreed it was its duty to help these misfits purge themselves."

Doc stood. "Sir, I don't want to take up any more of your time. You've been too kind already."

"Not at all. Can I expect to see you again?"

"I don't mind telling you that I'm very impressed with your philosophy. It's easy for me to see why it attracted Clint Stover." He opened the door as the bishop got up from the sofa. "It's all right," Doc said. "I'll show myself out." He took a step through the doors and stopped.

"Something else?" asked Lee.

"I was wondering about what you said about being an Indian agent."

"Yes?"

"Did you know there was an attack on a wagon train this morning?"

"No, I hadn't heard, but to be frank, I'm not surprised."

"I suppose it happens pretty regularly around here."

"I'm afraid that's true, but why are you concerned about this?"

"I treated some of the victims this morning. One little girl was killed. The attacks are so gruesome, and I wondered if you knew which tribe was doing it."

"It's no tribe, Doctor."

"No tribe?"

"It's a band of renegade Indians, about a hundred of them, and they're as ruthless as they are skilled riders and marksmen."

"I discovered they were using pistols instead of rifles. Where do you suppose they're getting so many handguns?"

"That's an interesting question, Doctor. I'll bring it up with the sheriff when I see him."

"Again, thank you, sir. I hope to see you again soon."

Doc left and closed the door behind him. At the opposite end of the hall, a man leaned on the wall and smoked a cigarette. As Doc approached him, he saw that the man wore a ratty gray wool suit and old riding boots. Thin black hair was greased neatly into place. A black string tie was slightly off center against the collar of a white cotton shirt. Doc judged him to be about twenty-five years old.

When Doc was within five feet of him, the man looked up. "Are you the doctor?" he asked.

Doc now recognized the face, protruding jaw, and blue eyes of John Wesley Hardin. To lawmen and gunslingers alike, Hardin was among the most feared men alive. He'd started killing when he was fifteen and hadn't stopped yet. Doc had heard in Kansas that Hardin actually faced down Wild Bill Hickock, the most famous lawman in the West.

"Yes, I'm a doctor," Doc said calmly.

"I got a problem, Doc."

"That so?"

"Yeah. I don't breathe so good."

Hardin took a last long drag on his cigarette and threw it on the floor. Doc noticed that he had a .44 pistol on each hip and a long knife tucked in his belt. His weaponry was the most impressive thing about him. He was pale and gaunt, and his suit barely clung to a painfully thin body.

"Tell me about your breathing problem, young man," Doc said.

Hardin took a deep breath and appeared to be annoyed. Doc remembered another story about Hardin. He'd killed a man who'd woken him up with a sneeze.

"It's like this, Doc," said the gunslinger in carefully measured tones. "I was out working hard, running and riding this morning, and since then I've been puffing and wheezing a lot. It's happened a few times before."

Doc was reluctant to recommend a phony elixir to such a dangerous and choleric man. He said, "You probably just need some rest. The air up here is not what you're used to, and I'm sure you'll be fine again once you get back home."

"How'd you know I'm not from around here?"

"The bishop told me he had guests, and I presumed you were one of them."

"Have I seen you someplace before?"

"I don't think so."

"You ever been to Abilene?" Hardin asked.

"I might have passed through."

The killer fixed Doc in a stare almost as lethal as the guns on his hips.

"Got to be going," said Doc. "Take care of yourself, drink liquids, and get lots of rest."

"Thanks, Doc."

Hardin turned and walked up the hall, stopped, turned, and quickly went through a door to his right. Doc managed to peek through the door before it closed behind Hardin. Seated at a round table was a big, heavyset man wearing a tuxedo and a stovepipe hat. Across from him was a tall, angular fellow wearing a round-brimmed hat with the words "Assistant Deputy" embroidered on it. Their faces were as familiar to Doc as Hardin's had been: Rowdy Joe Lowe and Dave Mather.

Doc left the mansion and climbed up on the springbroard

bench of his Studebaker. He took the reins in his hand and was about to slap Judith's rump, when he suddenly stopped, laid the reins on the floor, climbed down, and went around to the rear. He opened the trap door, removed a .44 pistol, inspected it, and then placed it on the seat next to him for the ride back to town. He felt better just knowing that it was there.

CHAPTER TEN

"Jesus, Molly, how do you expect me to know a thing like that?"

"I don't know, Raider, you seem to know a lot about things around here."

Raider blushed and said, "I reckon it's always been called Colorado."

"Oklahoma, Colorado . . . the places all have such funny names. They must be Indian names."

"Why do you say that?"

"Anybody who would call themselves Brown Deer or Mountain Cloud would name a place Colorado."

"Oh yeah, smarty pants, what are the cities called in England?"

"There's Devonshire, Twickenham, names like that."

"I think I'd rather have Indian names. Colorado sounds a hell of a lot better than Twickenham." They both laughed. "And I bet they don't have no Rocky Mountains in England, do they?"

"I never saw *any* mountains in England."

"You'd better get used to seeing them, because we're going to be in them for a long time from here on in."

"Will we see more Indians?"

"Reckon so, but probably not for a spell. We'll be spending the night in Denver. That's a big city. After that, we cut across the corner of Wyoming and get to Utah."

"Wyoming?" she said sarcastically.

"That's right, young lady, and I happen to think Wyoming's a fine name. Keep your sass to yourself." They laughed again.

Molly asked, "As long as we're so close to Danvers, do you think I could drive for a little while?"

"It's Denver. And no, you can't."

"How come?"

"These are big, strong horses, Molly, and we're going to be on crowded streets very soon."

"Please."

"No."

"You didn't think I could shoot, either, but I was pretty good, wasn't I?"

Raider scowled at her. His stare remained unbroken as he lifted his hand and slowly passed the reins across his body to her hands.

"I knew you'd see it my way."

She smiled and took the reins from him. The horses sensed the change and charged ahead erratically, veering to the right, where the road was rutted.

"What in the name of St. Bartholomew is going on up there?" Agnes screamed. "You been nipping at that hootch again, cowboy?"

"No, damn it, Molly's just showing off another of her many talents."

"I see." Agnes laughed. "Molly, honey, give the cowboy back the reins before we all get sick back here."

"Oh, please," Molly begged. "I'm just learning. I'll be good at it in no time. You'll see."

Agnes and Molly argued while Raider looked ahead along the trail. They were high up, and hills stretched out in every direction. He'd been to Denver before and figured that they were about a half hour from the city. He was about to turn and announce it, when a thin line of white smoke rising between two of the hills captured his attention. It was followed by several short puffs. He reached over and grabbed the reins from Molly.

"We're getting out of here," he said.

"What are you talking about?"

"*Hee-yah,*" Raider shouted as he slapped the reins over the horses' flanks as hard as he could. The wagon bolted forward, and Molly almost fell out.

"Sorry," Raider said.

"Damn it, cowboy," Agnes shouted. "Take the reins from her before she gets us all killed."

"He already has," Molly said.

"Then slow down, cowboy."

"If I slow down, Agnes, those Indians on the horizon will shut that big mouth of yours for good."

"Real Indians?" Molly gasped.

"In the hills," Raider said. "I seen their signals, and they'll be over the ridge any second now. Let's just hope we get far enough away so that they won't bother with us."

Molly inched closer to him on the bench. "I'm scared," she said.

Raider's face was a picture of intensity. His eyes were fixed straight ahead, and his clenched fists gripped the reins tightly.

A bride in the back of the wagon started crying.

"What is it, honey?" Agnes asked.

"I never should have left London."

"Don't worry, doll, everything will be okay. I promise

you." Agnes looked out the rear flap and saw a band of Indians come over a ridge a mile behind them. "There they are," she yelled.

"I'm scared," said one of the brides. "I've heard terrible stories about what Indians do to women."

"The cowboy'll get us out of it," Agnes said. "He's a good man. This is nothing new to him."

"What if he doesn't?" asked the girl.

"We have guns. We'll fight. I can shoot, and Lord knows the cowboy and that little girl up there with him can probably shoot better than any red man."

"But suppose they do come after us and catch up," one of the girls said. "Suppose we can't shoot good enough to stop them. If they catch us . . . if they catch *me* . . . what should I do?"

Agnes put her hands firmly on the girl's shoulders and looked deep into her eyes. "Point one of these guns at your head and pull the trigger," she said.

All the brides began to cry.

"Take it easy," Agnes said. "We'll get out of this." She peeled open the rear flap and peered out. "So far it looks clear, cowboy," she shouted to Raider.

He grunted and continued to urge the Percherons on. Then a cloud of dust rose from the road and vanished high above the horizon.

"They're coming, cowboy," Agnes yelled. "Put a move on!"

"*Whoa!*" Raider shouted, pulling hard on the reins. He leaped from the wagon, grabbed Molly's hand, and pulled her down with him. They ran to the rear.

"Have you gone nuts?" Agnes shrieked. "They're gaining on us."

"Drive," Raider said.

"What?"

"Drive, God damn it. There's no way those girls are going to hold off redskins while me and Molly are up front. At least we'll have a fighting chance with us back here."

Agnes took the reins while Raider loaded every weapon he could find. The wagon forged forward. Raider glanced out the back and saw that the Indians were now about a half mile away.

He turned to Molly and said, "I'm going to leave these guns between us. They're all loaded, so don't stop to reload. When you finish with one, pick up the next and keep on shooting. Use the pistols and leave the heavy stuff to me."

Molly nodded.

"Are you okay?" he asked.

She managed a faint smile.

"You ever shoot at anyone?"

"No."

"It'll be hard, but you have a right."

"My father was a lawman. When I was a little girl, he handed me my first gun and said, 'This is the most dangerous thing in the world. It's also the best way to protect yourself. Use it if you ever need to.' I'm not afraid, Raider."

"Good. Take your time and just pretend it's a tin can you're shooting at. Aim for the belly button because that always goes where its owner goes."

"Okay."

"And don't shoot till I tell you to."

They lay on their stomachs and lifted the rear flap. The Indians were drawing near. Raider glanced over at Molly. She held a .44 tightly with both hands, and her eyes were trained on the attackers. Suddenly, a dozen redskins broke away from the pack and sprinted for the wagon.

"This is it," Raider said in a calm voice. "Good luck, kid."

When the Indians were within two hundred feet, Raider shouted, "Now!"

He aimed his 30-30 and fired a round as Molly squeezed off two from her .44. Three red men hit the ground; one's skull was crushed beneath the hooves of his own horse.

The others kept coming, firing an occasional arrow but concentrating on overtaking and stopping the wagon. Raider flawlessly picked off his targets, but Molly was having trouble. One of the charging red men was now within twenty feet of her. Raider spotted him out of the corner of his eye and let loose a volley of shots at everyone in range, including the one closing in on Molly. He took the bullet in his gut but stayed on his horse. The animal, out of control, pounded even faster toward the rear of the wagon, nostrils flaring and foam flying from the corners of its mouth.

Molly was hypnotized by the dead Indian who continued to close the gap between them. Her eyes were glued to the charging corpse. Then his horse stumbled and the dead rider's head flopped back, with a steady stream of blood pouring from the mouth. Molly covered her eyes. An Indian who'd come abreast of his slain brother removed an arrow from his pouch, placed it in his bow, and aimed. Raider was out of shells and had no time to reload. He picked up a knife and threw it. It stuck the bowman in the throat, and blood gushed from his neck; he gripped his stallion's mane to keep from falling, and his crazed eyes bored holes into Molly. She screamed.

"Shoot the son of a bitch," Raider yelled.

She fired. The Indian's deerskin tunic filled with blood, but his eyes remained open. She fired three more times before he toppled from his horse in a lifeless heap, joining his brother on the ground in a mass of blood, sand, and intestines.

The attack was over.

"It's okay," Raider said, "they're gone."

Molly looked up as if she hadn't known he was there, fell into his arms, and sobbed uncontrollably.

"Take it easy, little lady," Raider said, patting her back. "You did just fine. Your daddy taught you good. He'd be right proud of you, just like I am."

CHAPTER ELEVEN

Molly was almost asleep in the hotel, when she heard a knock at the door. She rolled over and ignored it.

"Come on, Molly," shouted Raider, "I know you're in there."

She got out of bed, put on a robe, and went to the door. When she opened it, she saw Raider, Agnes, and the other brides.

"Come on, honey," Ann said. "It's just past suppertime. You don't want to turn in already. There's a whole new city out there, and Agnes is going to show us around a little."

"That's sweet, Ann, but it was a bloody tough day, and I think I'd better get some sleep."

Raider interrupted. "We know it's been a rough day for you, Molly, but that's why we're here, to thank you for being as brave and as good with a gun as you were." He pulled a bouquet of roses from behind his back and sheepishly extended them to her.

Her eyes lit up like those of a little girl. "These are for me?" she squealed, grabbing them without waiting for an answer. "Thank you so much. You're all so nice."

"That's not all," said Agnes.

"Right." Ann giggled. "The girl who helped save our lives is worth more than that."

She and Agnes stepped aside, and two of the brides handed Molly a box. Molly tore it open as fast as she could, pulled out a silk kimono, and held it up in front of her.

"It's the nicest one this side of Hong Kong," Agnes said. "It's from all of us."

Molly kissed and hugged everybody except Raider, who stood off in a corner and watched with a fatherly smile.

"Well," said Ann to Molly, "you certainly look wide awake now. Let's go out and paint the bloody town red."

"Thanks anyway," Molly said, "but I really don't want to. All I want is a nice, long bath, to get into my nightie, and to go to bed. Please understand." She smiled, kissed them again, and pranced down the hall toward the bath.

"Well," Agnes said, "I guess we should go. See you later, cowboy."

Raider went to his room, where he sat on the bed and cleaned his gun. After a few minutes, he said aloud to himself, "What the hell am I doing? I haven't had a good lay in weeks, I'm in a big city, and all I'm doin' is sitting by myself and cleaning out the wrong gun." He grabbed his leather jacket and threw it over his shoulder, paused briefly in front of the mirror to run his fingers through his hair, stepped into the hall, and walked to the top of the stairs. He stopped and turned as he heard Molly come out of the bathroom.

"There you are," she said. "I'm so glad. I just remembered that I forgot to especially thank you for the flowers."

"Oh, don't even think about it," Raider said.

He openly ravished her with his eyes. She'd rushed from the tub to see him and was still wet, which caused the silk kimono to cling to her body. Her breasts and erect nipples were clearly visible through the flimsy white garment. It was tied with a sash around the waist, which left a good part of her chest open to scrutiny. Wet strands of hair clung to her face.

She noticed Raider staring and said, "Oh, how do you like it on me?"

She spread her arms to their fullest, which not only brought the garment tighter to her breasts but also revealed her long legs. Raider had become so protective of her recently and had been so amused at her innocence, he'd forgotten how beautiful she was.

"It's mighty pretty," he said, "and so are you."

"Why, thank you," Molly said. She put her arms around his shoulders and hugged him. "Thank you for everything."

Raider felt a familiar stirring in his groin, and he shuffled his feet in an attempt to hide the bulge in his pants. "Go on now," he said. "Get off to bed."

"Okay," she said, bouncing down the hall, her buttocks undulating beneath the silk fabric.

"Jesus Christ," Raider said to himself when she was gone. "I got to find me a woman before I do something I'll regret."

He'd been in Denver before and knew exactly where he was heading. Some of the best nights in his life had been spent in the Golden Nugget, a saloon not far from the hotel.

He settled in at the bar and ordered a drink, looked over the crowd, and smiled. It was one of the few places in the West where there were as many women as men, women of every size and shape, old and young, plain and fancy, and, most important, all available.

He ordered a second drink and scouted the females in the crowd. Before he could make a choice, a voice next to him said, "Buy me a drink, cowboy?" It was a blond who'd slid into the seat next to him.

"Sure," he said, taking in her well-proportioned body. She had vivid red lips, wide green eyes, and a pink tongue that kept darting out between pearly white teeth.

"The usual, Stretch," she said to the barkeep. She returned her attention to Raider and said, "Well, handsome, what's your name?"

"Raider."

"Raider. I like it. It's got a nice ring."

"Always served me okay."

"I'll bet it has. Why don't you tell me what you're doing in Denver. It's a long way from Arkansas."

"Hold on a minute," he said. "I never said I was from Arkansas."

"Men are my business, cowboy. I can place any man I meet in his home state as easy as placing a foreigner in his home country. Matter of fact, most of the time I can get the city within twenty square miles."

"No shit?"

"That's right."

"Okay, tell what city I'm from."

"A Fayetteville boy if I ever heard one. Your cowboy act don't cover up nothing."

"I'll be damned. That's really something."

"So tell me, good looking, why Denver?"

"Just passing through."

"On the way to . . ."

"Salt Lake City."

"You ain't an Arkansas Mormon, are you?"

"Shit, no."

"Too bad. That's about the only sort of man left I haven't screwed."

"What makes you think you're going to screw me?"

"Like I told you, Raider, men are my business. There's not much thinking involved."

Raider laughed and followed her toward the stairs, his eyes glued to her full, bouncy ass and shapely legs.

He was distracted momentarily by an argument at one of the tables. He stopped.

"I tell you for the last time," shouted a big man who was standing, "I was leaving, anyway, and that's the only reason I gave him my seat. I ain't afraid of any man alive, not even him."

"That's why you didn't come back in here till two days later, after he was out of town, right?" a heckler yelled from a few tables away.

"Damn it, I told you boys I was taking inventory over at my store."

"And you ain't afraid of him?" another heckler shouted.

"If he was here now, I'd tell him to his face."

"If he was here now, you'd be back at your store doing inventory."

Raider and the blond went up the stairs as the man who'd been on the receiving end of the taunts went for one of his tormentors' throats.

"By the way," she said as they reached her room, "my name's Bonnie."

"I like it," Raider said.

"Always served me okay," she replied with a wide grin. Then, without saying another word, she began filling a tub with hot water.

"What were those boys arguing about?" Raider asked.

"Who cares? All they ever do is argue."

"No, they were talking about somebody they seemed to think was pretty tough."

"I'm not surprised. They've been talking about him ever since he left."

"Who?"

"Jesse James."

"You're pulling my leg."

"It's no big deal. He might be tough, but he's got a limp cock."

"You fucked Jesse James?"

"Yup, and it sure as hell wasn't too exciting. The whole thing lasted about two minutes."

Raider laughed. "How do you know it really was him?"

"It was him."

"I traveled all over this country, Bonnie, and if I had a buck for every guy I met who claimed to know Jesse James or to have ridden with him, I'd be a rich man. I don't suppose you charged him the full price, with him being so famous and all."

"I worked a long time to be a fifteen-dollar lay, Raider. Nobody gets out cheaper than that."

"Well, I still don't believe it was Jesse James. Why the hell would he be in Denver?"

"I didn't ask, but I'm sure it was he."

"How?"

"Who the hell else from Clay County, Missouri, would be in Denver?"

"How'd you know that's where he came from?"

"I knew it the minute he opened his mouth."

"Oh yeah." Raider laughed. "I forgot about that."

She reached behind and unbuttoned her dress. It dropped to the floor, revealing a scarlet chemise. She removed it and was naked. Her breasts were even larger than they'd appeared, and her nipples were huge, her belly full.

"Well, what do you think?" she asked.

"I think I'm in for a hell of a night."

"I think you're right." She moved toward him and unbuttoned the top buttons of his denim shirt. He reached for the bottom buttons, but she stopped him. "I'll take care of everything," she said.

When he was out of his shirt, she ran her fingers through the hair on his chest and brushed her lips lightly across his nipples. She kissed his stomach and darted her tongue in and out of his navel while unbuckling his belt and undoing the buttons on his pants. She pulled off a boot and sock, and then repeated it with his other foot. She dropped his pants to the ground, leaving him in his white cotton underpants. She pulled them off and admired his pulsating erection.

"Jesus Christ," she said, "I ought to charge double for that big bugger."

Raider laughed proudly and pulled her toward him.

"Not yet," she said. "I can tell from the look in your eye you've been on the trail too long. Let's take care of you nice and quick before we do it the way it's supposed to be done."

"All right," said Raider, a little disappointed but not about to argue with her.

She dropped to her knees, and all of Raider's disappointment instantly disappeared into her warm mouth. She circled the head of his penis for a few minutes, her tongue gently massaging it. She moved her head forward and then back, taking more of him into her mouth with each movement. Raider felt his knees grow weak and was afraid that his legs wouldn't support him much longer. He needn't have worried. His orgasm hit him like a tidal wave, and she swallowed his come like a child enjoying a lollipop.

"How's that?" she asked, looking up.

He fell on the bed. "Fantastic. Come over here."

"Not yet," she said. She went to the tub and poured in more hot water, making steam rise into the room. "Okay," she said, "get in."

Raider, who was basically a meat-and-potatoes man when it came to sex, said, "Can't we just do it again in bed?"

"The heat," she said. "It gets you up faster and makes you last longer."

"That a fact?"

"I know men. That's my business."

Raider climbed into the tub, and Bonnie sat on the edge of the bed. She crossed her legs and smiled. The water's warmth loosened Raider's tired muscles, and only the sight of her huge, provocative breasts kept him from falling asleep.

After a minute she purred, "Ready, Raider?"

He stood in the tub. She picked up a towel and slowly and deliberately dried him. When she was done, she looked into his face and said, "It's all yours. Let's see what you can do with it."

Raider grinned like a cat who'd been left to mind the bird. He picked her up in his arms and kissed her neck as he carried her to the bed where he placed her on silk sheets. They met in a wet kiss. He lay down next to her, and she pulled him close, her dexterous tongue exploring every corner of his mouth. She took his hand and placed it on one of her breasts. Its firmness was remarkable: white marble. Raider squeezed it and flicked his fingers over her nipple, which became rigid. He drew imaginary circles around her areola with his fingernails until the nipple was rock-hard and then drew it into his mouth while his hand toyed with her other breast. He glanced at her. Her eyes were closed, and contentment was written all over her face.

He kneeled on the bed and pressed both breasts together, one nipple stimulating the other. She smiled, put her hands around his buttocks, and pulled him closer. His erection had returned to its full glory, and she engulfed it between her magnificent mammaries. She clasped her tits and moved his hard penis between them as though he'd entered her. Now it was his turn to close his eyes and smile.

Ordinarily, Raider didn't enjoy extended foreplay. There

was an added problem this night, however. Despite the presence of the voluptuous woman beneath him, he was having trouble getting Jesse James off his mind. Everybody at Pinkerton took James's career personally ever since his gang had murdered several operatives, and although Raider had never met him, he felt an intense rivalry. He was determined to show Bonnie that he was better than James in every possible way.

He rolled off her, and then went back to mouth probing, with their sweaty bodies welded together. Raider slid his hand down to a vagina that dripped with natural sexual lubrication. This was no run-of-the-mill whore. She was legitimately excited by her customer. He wanted to plunge in but resisted and instead toyed with her vulva, feeling it grow hotter and juicier. She pushed him on his back and attempted to impale herself on his penis, but he was so enjoying seeing her desperate for him that he foiled her attempt by sitting up and meeting her with a kiss. He continued the foreplay and decided, based upon her passionate responses, that Jesse James couldn't have been half this good.

He eventually fell on his back, and Bonnie lowered herself onto his erection. She moved very slowly, and he was surprised how tight an experienced pro could be. She matched her descent with a circular motion of her hips, and the sensation it created in Raider's groin was so intense that only the thought of Jesse James's two-minute stint with her kept him from coming. He'd last long enough to make her forget that Jesse James ever existed.

His hands cupped her buttocks as his eyes feasted on the melonlike breasts dangling between their bodies. She reached behind, took one of his hands, and placed his index finger on her swollen clitoris. She picked up the pace, and he matched her gyrations, his finger never losing contact with her clit. She moaned as she neared orgasm. Raider relaxed a bit and prepared for his own eruption. Then, to his surprise, she stopped.

"What the hell's going on?" Raider asked. "Don't tell me my time's up."

"Hold on, cowboy, we're just getting to the good part."

"I liked the part we was just in."

Employing a double-jointedness Raider had never seen before, she pointed both legs up and out without disengaging. She supported herself on her hands and easily spun around so that her back was to him.

"You like that?" she asked.

"Yup."

She slowly rotated a full three hundred sixty degrees, and they laughed. Raider sat up the best he could, reached around, and found her magnificent breasts. The nipples hadn't softened a bit. She energetically moved up and down, her body throwing off tremendous heat. He was so busy watching her sexual antics, he'd almost forgotten his own gratification. A wave of pleasure surged through his body, and he fell on his back and enjoyed the muscular contractions of her vagina. They lasted almost a minute before she screamed at the same moment of Raider's release.

Later, she lay with her head on his chest. "I haven't come with a paying customer in God knows how long," she said, sounding tired.

"Was I better than Jesse James?" Raider asked proudly.

She grinned. "You make him look like he has no balls." She sat up. "But why such a big interest in Jesse James? He may not be much in the sack, Raider, but if you ever meet that boy, you'd better be on your toes."

Raider laughed and perched on the edge of the bed.

"Don't go," Bonnie said.

"I have to, little lady. You might say I'm working."

"You staying in town long?"

"Leaving in the morning."

"Wouldn't you know it?"

He pulled on his denims and rifled his pockets for cash.

"Forget it," Bonnie said.

"What do you mean?"

"Forget the money."

"I thought you charged everybody the full fare, no matter what."

"This one's on me. Besides, I charged Jesse James double."

Raider roared, bent down, and kissed her on the lips. "So long, honey. Maybe I'll see you again someday."

"Whether you do or not, I can promise you one thing."

"What's that?"

"Next time I hear a Fayetteville boy, I'll be right sure to introduce myself."

He walked back to the hotel in a light drizzle. It was nearly two, but he wasn't sleepy and didn't feel like going up to his room. He went over to a clerk behind the desk and said, "Howdy. The name's Raider. I'm staying here as a paying guest."

"Room 11."

"Right you are. I've been on the road a spell, and it feels good to be in a real town, only I ain't quite ready to pack it in yet."

"Well, the clerk said, "the Golden Nugget is a good place for gents who've been on the road." He winked awkwardly.

"I just come back from the Golden Nugget, where I met me a mighty fine little lady." Raider threw back his shoulders like a barnyard rooster and flapped his wings in triumph.

The clerk laughed and then fell silent and scrutinized him.

"Something wrong?" Raider asked.

"Are you a Pinkerton agent, Mr. Raider?"

Raider was taken aback by the question. Was the clerk another operative? "Pinkerton?" he said.

"Yes, sir. You know, a detective."

"Where'd you get a crazy idea like that?"

"From Jesse James."

"Jesse James told you I was a Pinkerton?"

"Not exactly."

"Well, how about being a little exact?"

"You see, Mr. Raider, him and Frank and that other fellow, Cole Younger, were all in the hotel this week. I waited on them every night while they sat here in the lobby and drank and played cards. One night Mr. James, he says to me, 'Kid, don't trust the next fellow who stays in my room.' Well, I ask him how come, and he says that Pinkerton is so hot on his trail that nine times out of ten a Pinkerton detective sleeps in the same bed he sleeps in the very next day."

"That a fact?"

"Sure is. He told me, too, that sometimes they even sleep with the same woman just to get information."

"Sounds farfetched to me," Raider said, suppressing a smile.

"I swear its true."

"Seems to me Pinkerton would catch somebody as bad as Jesse James if they were that close to him."

"Shucks, Mr. James wasn't so bad at all. He says it's the newspapers and Pinkerton that make him out to be bad."

"That so?"

"Yup. He told me that he shot off one of his fingers while cleaning his gun about a month or so ago and that he couldn't even see a doctor. He darn near bled to death."

"Hell of a shame," Raider said.

"Sure is," said the clerk.

"Well, it looks like Jesse James was wrong this time. I'm just a cowpuncher heading west."

"If you say so."

"You don't have to believe me, son, but how many Pinkerton detectives you know who dress like me or talk like me? I thought all of those boys wore fancy suits, rode fancy horses, and talked like sissies."

"I never thought about it like that before."

"I reckon I'm tired, after all. Think I'll turn in."

"Good night, Mr. Raider."

"Good night, son."

CHAPTER TWELVE

Doc seldom got nervous. Countless Pinkerton assignments had seen to that. He'd had his back to the wall more times than he cared to remember, yet he was still in perfect health.

For that reason, the butterflies in his stomach caused more discomfort than they would to the average man. In a few minutes, he'd be heading for the Salt Lake Saloon. Word had quickly spread that the saloon would be open late and that all the bishop's "guests" would be there. Naturally, Doc planned to be there, too, although he questioned the logic of being the only Pinkerton in the midst of the nation's most talented, feared, and dangerous outlaws.

Noise from the saloon spilled into the street, and Doc could hear the revelry from a distance. He reached inside his jacket and patted his Diamondback. He'd checked it a dozen times since dinner and knew that he'd probably keep checking it until he was safely back in his room.

He reached the saloon's entrance, took a deep breath, and went inside. The crowd was exactly as promised, and it seemed that every photograph Pinkerton had ever sent him had come to life in that room. He moved slowly through the crowd to the bar, ordered a drink, and then worked his way back across the packed floor in search of a table. Most of them were taken, and at least ten were the scene of high-stakes poker games.

Doc now knew that Beckett hadn't exaggerated. It was a rogue's gallery of the infamous. He saw Mather and Lowe again, recognized the Clantons, the McClowerys, Johnny Ringo, Kid Cummings, Bill Raynor, and Bill Longley. Everywhere he looked was a man more notorious than the next. At a table in the center of the saloon sat John Wesley Hardin. He was by himself. Hardin had the reputation of being the outlaw's outlaw, feared as much by his peers as he was by lawmen. He never needed an excuse to kill.

As Doc passed his table, Hardin looked up and said, "Hold on a minute. Is that you, Doc?"

Doc turned slowly and nodded.

"Damn, I'm glad I caught you. What are you drinking?"

"Scotch, straight up."

Hardin grabbed a waitress by the elbow. "You heard the man. Hop to it." He said to Doc, "Sit down, come on, join me."

Doc took a chair across from Hardin, who was much more cordial than at their first meeting. The waitress brought Doc's drink, and Hardin raised his glass.

"To Doc Weatherbee, one hell of a smart guy."

"Well, I thank you," Doc said after downing his original drink and turning to the fresh one, "but what makes you think I'm so intelligent?"

"My chest. I done what you told me to do, spent the last few days resting. I feel a hell of a lot better."

"I'm certainly glad to hear that Mr. . . . ."

"Hardin, John Wesley Hardin."

"Always glad to help my fellow man, Mr. Hardin. You remember that."

"I will. Fellows like me usually don't live too long. Our

time comes up pretty quick. That don't really bother me much, but while I'm around, I'd just as soon feel as good as I can."

Doc realized that the conversation had turned more than casual. "I'm not quite sure I understand," he said, being careful not to anger Hardin. "What exactly do you mean 'fellows like you'?"

"It's not important. Anyhow, I think I might be doing some riding tomorrow. What do you reckon I should do if I start having pain again?"

"Same thing, Mr. Hardin. It's all you can do until you get back home. The respiratory system is a funny thing."

Doc took out an Old Virginia cheroot, lit it, and then offered one to Hardin. As he reached for it, Doc saw Jacques, the leader of the wagon train that had been ambushed, heading for the table.

"Dr. Weatherbee," he said, "I saw you sitting here and thought it would be a good time to answer your questions."

Doc glanced at Hardin, who stared into his glass of tequila.

"Of course, Jacques," Doc said. "Always happy to discuss your health." The Frenchman seemed confused as Doc got up and grabbed him by the elbow. Doc said to Hardin, "Looks like I have more work to do. Thanks for the drink. Hope to see you again soon."

As soon as they were in the street, Jacques said, "I told you yesterday, Doctor, that there is nothing wrong with my health, but I did promise to answer your questions when you were finished treating my friends. You did a wonderful job, and I thank you. *Merci*."

"The truth is, Jacques, I asked you just about everything I need to know."

"I see." He hung his head.

"Is something wrong?"

"*Oui*. I am very worried. There were two wagon trains leaving from the East."

"And?"

"And the second one will travel along the same road tomorrow. I am concerned that it too, will be attacked."

"Are they Frenchmen?"

"*Oui*, mostly women and children. If they meet those Indians, they will be slaughtered like animals."

"I don't think there's any reason to worry, Jacques. Indians rarely attack in the same place so soon. They'll be worried that the law will be after them."

"I've learned that the law does not take very good care of immigrants, Doctor."

"I suppose it doesn't."

"Well, thank you for your time. I hope I didn't spoil your evening."

"No, not at all."

Jacques walked away, and Doc looked in the window of the saloon. Through the thick clouds of smoke he saw Hardin, unchanged, staring into his tequila. He decided that he'd pressed his luck far enough and went back to the King's Hotel for a bath and a good night's sleep.

Raider adjusted the right rein and guided the horses around a curve in the road. Agnes was sitting stoically on the seat next to him. The temperature was close to ninety, and the effects of the long trip had taken a toll on everyone.

"I'll tell you a fact, cowboy," Agnes said. "I was beginning to think we'd never see Utah."

"Well, this is it. Look around and enjoy it."

"I guess we'll hit Salt Lake tomorrow."

"That's what I'm figuring."

"I'll miss these girls, won't you?"

"I reckon." He couldn't admit that he'd grown fond

and protective of the brides, especially Molly. They'd become the daughters he'd never had.

"What'll you do when this is over, Raider?"

"Don't rightly know."

They rode along quietly for another few minutes. Molly and the other girls were chatting gleefully in the back. Raider took a handkerchief from his pocket and mopped his brow.

"You mind?" Agnes asked, extending her hand. Raider handed the handkerchief to her, and she wiped her face vigorously.

"What do you make of all this Jesse James nonsense?" she asked. "Seems like we've heard nothing else since leaving Colorado."

"It seems that way."

"Think he's really around here?"

"Yup."

"I've heard it all before, only I got to admit that a lot of folks seem to believe it this time."

"I don't know, Agnes," Raider said. "I may not be the smartest dude in the world, but sometimes I get mighty strong feelings, and one of them right now is that me and Mr. James might come face to face real soon."

"You scared?"

"Nope."

"You're right, Raider. You ain't the smartest dude in the world."

They came around a bend and saw a circle of covered wagons in a clearing. Raider pulled the wagon into the circle and stopped. The brides hopped out, and Ann approached a young woman from the wagon train. She extended her hand and said, "I'm Ann. How are you?"

The young woman meekly clasped Ann's hand and replied, *"Je ne comprend pas."*

"Oh," Ann said. She said to the other brides, "They're

French. I feel closer to home now." The girls laughed, and Ann returned her attention to the French woman. *"Je m'appelle Ann,"* she said.

The other woman smiled. "Oh, *je m'appelle Marie.*"

A tall, muscular man joined the group. "Welcome strangers," he said.

Raider stepped forward and shook his hand. "How do you do?"

"Fine, thank you. If you folks are looking for a place to spend the night, you're welcome to stay here."

"Will you be heading for Salt Lake in the morning?" Raider asked.

"Passing just north. We're going to the Northwest. Another group of our countrymen left a few days ahead of us, and we'll all rendezvous in Oregon."

"Well," Raider said, "we're only going as far as Salt Lake City, but we might as well stick together."

"Tres bien," the man said. "Make yourselves at home."

CHAPTER THIRTEEN

Raider estimated that they were within a mile of Salt Lake City, and he was filled with anticipation. His throat was dry; the sun was at its zenith in the sky. He looked around at the cracking, arid ground and then up at the mountains in the distance. It wasn't unique, yet Utah seemed to possess a special majesty.

He thought of Doc, and a sly grin found his lips. He looked forward to their reunion like two kids on the first day of school. As much as he'd enjoyed the company of Agnes and the brides, he missed the rough-and-tumble times he and Doc had often shared. As much as he hated to admit it, he really liked his partner.

He knew that Doc had been in Salt Lake City for a while but had no idea what his assignment was. "I wonder what that rascal is up to," he muttered under his breath.

"How's that?" asked Agnes.

"I was just thinking out loud."

"About your detective business?"

"Yup."

"Well, at least you have something else to keep you busy."

"What does that mean?"

"You'll have another job right away."

"That's right."

"An old battle-ax like me don't find work that easy. I mean, who wants to hire an old lady?"

"You sure as hell do decent job, Agnes, I'll say that for you."

"Maybe I'll join up with Pinkerton." She laughed.

"That's all I need," Raider said, "you looking over my shoulder for the next twenty years."

"Maybe I have been a little tough on you, cowboy, but I had a job."

"I know, and I respect it."

"I'm sorry to see it all end. An old lady gets attached to people a lot faster than folks like you and the gals back there."

"You ain't so old, Agnes."

She smiled. "Thanks, Raider, I appreciate that."

He steered the wagon around a bend in the trail where it narrowed. They were the last of seven wagons following in a single file. They snaked through several more twists in the road until reaching a broad clearing. The lead wagon glided to a standstill, and the others followed. The driver of the first wagon climbed down from his bench and signaled Raider to pull abreast of him, which Raider did.

"This is where we must part, friend," the Frenchman said. "You must head south to the Salt Lake. It is no more than a mile."

"Right," Raider said. "It feels good to reach the end of a long, tough trip. It was good to know you. Take care. There's a lot of tough country between here and Oregon."

"We will. Godspeed to you."

They shook hands, and Raider returned to his wagon. As he reached it, a shot sounded. He whirled and saw blood spurt from the Frenchman's gut as he collapsed to the hard ground. Immediately, dozens of Indians swarmed over a ridge, screaming and firing at everything in sight.

"Come on, cowboy," Agnes screamed, "let's haul ass."

Raider watched as men, women, and children foolishly abandoned the line of wagons and ran helter-skelter, with the Indians picking them off at will. He heard the brides crying in the back, their wailing adding to the cacophony of sound. He wanted to stay and help the dying French.

"Damn it," Agnes shrieked, "you got a job to do, and if you don't do it right now, I will."

Raider leaped up onto the seat and grabbed the reins. A small group of attackers bore down on their right flank. Raider whipped his team, and the wagon bolted directly at them. He steered with one hand and fired with the other, managing to fell two Indians, but two others continued their charge. Raider held his ground, whipping the team relentlessly and holding them in a straight line. One attacker veered to the right, but the other could not, and the huge draft horses hit him full force, pounding his body and mount into the ground.

The remaining Indians concentrated on the French wagons and did not give chase. Still, Raider kept the horses steaming ahead until they came within view of the Great Salt Lake.

"There it is," Raider said, tugging on the reins and turning toward Agnes.

She didn't answer.

"Are you all right?" Raider asked, touching her. Then he saw two bullet wounds in her side: one just below the armpit, the other above the waist.

She was dead. Blood dripped to the floorboards, and a steady, slow series of red drops fell to the ground.

Raider looked up to see the brides staring at him. "Is she . . ."

"Afraid so. I guess that last Indian hit her before he veered off." He buried his head in his hands and shook it. "Goddamn savages," he muttered. He suddenly sat up straight and said, "Let's get back to town. I have to find the sheriff." The girls, who were all staring at Agnes, ignored him. "Come on," he growled, "we got to get help to those Frenchmen."

Ann looked up at him. "I can't get back in the wagon and ride with her dead like this. I just couldn't do it. She was like a mother to me."

"We have to bring her in for the undertakers," Raider said.

"I know," Ann said, crying softly, "but I just couldn't do it. Leave me here. I'll walk into town."

"Nobody's walking into town. Now that Agnes is gone, I got an obligation to look after you."

"Why don't we bury her ourselves?" one of the girls suggested.

"Takes too much time. Look, we'll leave her body out here. When we get to town, we'll have the undertaker ride out and bring her back."

The girls seemed satisfied, and so Raider dragged Agnes's body into a patch of grass at the side of the road. He stood over her and looked down.

"God damn it, Agnes," he said, "I should have guessed you'd go and do a dumb-ass thing like this." He removed his Stetson and said, "I liked you," then put it back on his head, turned, and climbed on the wagon. "Come on," he said to the brides, "get in. We got to see if we can help those people."

He drove into town, where he stopped in front of the sheriff's office, ran inside, and shouted, "A wagon train's been hit by Indians just north of here. It was full of Frenchmen."

"That so," said the sheriff, not looking up from the gun he was cleaning.

"Ain't you going to do something?"

"I reckon the red bastards are gone by now. That's the way they work. Happens all the time around here, mister. It ain't a big deal." He giggled "I'd like to help, but I'm sheriff of Salt Lake City, Utah. When the sheriff of France comes through, I'll be sure and let him know about it."

Raider stormed from the office and went to the wagon, where the girls stood out in the road.

"Let's go," he said. "I'm going to the hotel and get an old friend to help me. You girls can wait there until we get back."

He beat on a bell on the front desk until a clerk appeared. "What room is Doc Weatherbee in?" he barked.

"Number 5."

He was halfway up the stairs when the desk clerk shouted, "He's not in his room."

Raider stopped and slowly turned. "I don't have time to play games," he bellowed. "Where the hell is he?"

"Down the road at Mrs. Stover's. It's a white house with a little rose garden out front."

"Wait here," Raider said to the brides. "Have the clerk find the undertaker and send him out to get Agnes. I'll be back as soon as I can."

He ran outside and headed for Emily's house. He was almost there when he noticed her neighbor come out of his house and drive off in a two-wheeled dump cart. He thought the man's face was familiar, but forgot about it in his haste to find Doc. He charged up to Emily's door and burst in without knocking. He looked around but didn't see anyone. As he walked past the kitchen, someone pounced on him from behind a door, gripped him by the neck, and twisted him to the ground. Raider flipped himself over and faced his attacker.

"I should have guessed it was you," Doc said. "You're the only bastard rude enough to walk into a lady's house without knocking."

Raider's eyes opened wide. He grinned. "Sheet, it's you, Doc." Then he turned serious and said, "Listen, you son of a bitch, I got no time for bullshit. We was riding with a wagon train north of here, and it was hit by Indians. They slaughtered everybody, didn't even give them a chance to run away: kids, women, *everybody*."

"Were they Frenchmen?"

"How'd you know that?"

"It's not the first time."

"I want to get back out there and help them."

They scrambled to their feet, and Doc yelled, "Emily, I'll be back later. Another wagon train's been hit."

She appeared in the doorway and said, "Be careful." Then, to Raider, "I'm Emily."

He mumbled a greeting as he and Doc ran to the big covered wagon that had carried the brides across the country.

"Wait a minute," said Doc. "Let's take my wagon. I hate the way you drive."

"Not a chance," Raider said. "It'll take that old mule a week to get out there. Besides, we need room to bring back bodies."

Doc reluctantly agreed and pulled himself up onto the springboard bench. "Christ," he said, "this seat is full of blood."

"I know. They killed the old lady I was riding with."

"Sorry to hear it."

"Me, too. She was a good old bitch."

They reached the lake, and Raider looked at the spot where Agnes's body had been left.

"Well that's some service," he said.

"What?"

"That's where I left the old lady. Looks like the undertaker took care of things. Efficient son of a bitch."

"I'll remember that if I die here," Doc said.

They reached the clearing, where they were surrounded by the bloody bodies of Frenchmen.

"Jesus Christ," Doc said, "I've never seen anything like this. They're mostly women and kids."

"The red bastards," Raider snarled.

They looked up to see a little boy running toward them across the bloodstained field.

"*Monsieur, monsieur,*" the boy cried out loudly. He reached the wagon and tugged at Raider's sleeve.

"Take it easy, son," Raider said. "You're safe now." The boy continued pulling and tugging. "I think he's trying to tell us something," Raider said. "Let's follow."

They got down off the wagon and followed him to a man with black curly hair and a thick, black beard. He'd taken several bullets in the stomach, and a chunk of his side the size of a man's fist had been blown away. He was still conscious but could barely speak.

"We had no chance," he said in a thick French accent. "They shot us like dogs."

His head flopped to the side, and the boy screamed, "*Mon pere,*" as he threw his tiny arms around him.

Raider pulled the boy away as Doc bent down and put his ear to the man's chest.

"He's still alive," he said. "We have to get him back to town."

They surveyed the rest of the victims and found three others who were still alive. None spoke English. They placed them in the big wagon and headed for Doc Hastings's house.

As they entered town, Emily ran from her house and signaled for Raider to stop the wagon. He did, and she shouted, "I already fetched Doc Hastings. He's in here with me."

"Good girl," Doc said. "We got five of them."

Hastings came out and helped carry the injured people into the house. "It looks bad," he said when they got inside. "Is anything wrong with the little boy?"

"He's just scared," Doc said. "I think that fellow over there is his father."

Hastings looked at the man. "He's lost a lot of blood. I don't think he'll make it. And these three women have serious head wounds."

"Can't we do something for them?" Doc asked. "I'd really like to know what happened out there."

"I'll try, but right now I'd suggest praying."

Raider spoke up. "I knew I should have turned around. Those redskinned bastards must have been shooting them up for an hour. I should have stayed and helped."

"How?" asked Doc, "by getting yourself killed?"

"Excuse me, Mrs. Stover," Hastings said, "I'll need to use your sofa. I'll remove the bullets and try to stop the bleeding."

"Certainly."

"Emily," said Doc, "why don't you take the boy into the kitchen and fix him something to eat. He shouldn't be witness to this."

She took the youngster by the hand and led him away.

Hastings went to work, and Doc motioned for Raider to follow him into the bedroom.

"What the hell were you doing with those Frenchmen?" Doc asked after closing the door behind them. "Does Pinkerton know something you haven't told me?"

"Nope. We met them on the road last night and rode in with them."

"Where are you coming from?"

"New York."

"New York? You kidding me?"

"Hell, no. I come clear across country in a covered wagon."

"What were you doing?"

"Delivering mail-order brides."

Doc grinned. "No?"

"Yeah." Raider smiled, too.

"Well, you can tell me all about it later, and I'm sure you've got lots to tell."

"That's right."

"Right now we've got a case to work on."

"Shit, I just got here."

"Just in time."

"Tell me about the case."

"Jesus, I don't know where to start."

"Why don't you try the beginning," Raider said, borrowing a line Doc often used on him.

"Okay, joker. Salt Lake City is filled up with so many criminals, you wouldn't believe it."

"Big deal. There's lots of tough towns out west. It's no reason to call in Pinkerton."

"I'm not talking about the folks who live here, Raider. They're a bunch of Mormons. The bad ones have been filtering in over the past month."

"Like who?"

"Hardin, Ringo, Lowe, Mather, McClowery, Clanton, Raynor, Longley, Cummings, even some gangs from back east."

"How about James?"

"Not yet."

"Well, you should be expecting him real soon."

"How do you figure?"

"We've been one step behind him since we left Missouri. Every town we hit was buzzing because Jesse James just passed through. Fact is, I slept in the same hotel room as him and banged his whore.''

''That's something to be proud of,'' Doc said sarcastically.

''I should be, damn it. She said I was better in the sack than he was.''

''Raider, do you want to talk about sex or do you want to work on this case with me?''

''Sorry. So what the hell are all these gunslingers doing here?''

''If I knew that, I wouldn't need your help. I figure it might have something to do with all the recent Indian attacks.''

''That don't make a bucket of sense to me. Why would the biggest outlaws in the country come out here to hit wagon trains and split it with Indians?''

''I don't think that's it, Raider. Tell me, these Indians, did they use arrows?''

''No.''

''Rifles?''

''A few; mostly handguns.''

''So how do you suppose a gang of Indians got hold of so many pistols?''

''Some white man's selling to them, I guess.''

''Or lots of white men.''

''Still don't add up. Hell, how much money can they make selling guns?''

''If they sell enough of them, the country could have one hell of an Indian uprising on its hands.''

''It sounds farfetched to me, Doc.''

''Maybe, but it's the best I can come up with at the moment.''

They walked into the kitchen and sat at the table, where the boy was eating a sandwich.

"Doc," Emily whispered, "what's going on? I'm scared."

"I don't know, honey, but I have a feeling it's just getting started."

"Excuse me," Raider said to Emily, "but do I know the name Stover from somewhere?"

"Emily's husband, Clint, was my first partner with Pinkerton, Raider. You've probably heard me speak of him."

"I sure have. I always wanted to meet him."

"My husband passed away several years ago," Emily said.

"I'm sorry."

"He was a wonderful man, Mr. Raider, and if the way Doc speaks of you is any indication, you're pretty wonderful yourself."

"Is that so?" said Raider, glancing at Doc, who seemed embarrassed. "Tell me something, Emily, do you happen to know a Mormon fellow by the name of Edmonds?"

"Daniel Edmonds? We've met a few times. Why?"

"Could you tell me what he's like?"

She laughed. "You might call him eccentric."

"Pardon?"

"Eccentric," Doc said. "It's what you call a fellow who's too rich to call crazy."

Raider thought a moment before saying, "I guess that explains why he ordered six mail-order brides."

"He did what?" Emily asked.

"He sent to England for six brides. They're over at the hotel right now. I'm supposed to bring them up to his place."

"It's the biggest house in town," Emily said. "You can't miss it."

"I reckon I'd better go do it," Raider said, heading for the door.

"He really ordered six brides?" Doc asked, his voice mirroring his incredulity.

"I swear it."

"And you brought them all the way from New York?"

"Yup, through floods and Indian raids and lots of other troubles."

"I think me and you got to have a long talk later, partner." He laughed loudly.

"Not much to talk about, Doc. The fact is that—"

Hastings entered the room and said, "I've done what I can. The boy's father will need lots of rest and care, and even then his chances aren't very good."

"And the others?" Doc asked.

"Dead."

"I'd better have the undertaker come over and pick them up," said Emily.

"We'll have to do it ourselves," Hastings said.

"Why?"

"Stan, the undertaker, is out of town a couple of days visiting kin."

"That can't be," Raider insisted. "He already picked up Agnes."

"I don't know about any Agnes," Hastings said, "but I do know that Stan is out of town. He left me the key to his shop so I'd be able to store bodies."

"Does he have an assistant?" Doc asked.

"Nope, just he and his wife. Speaking of wives, mine'll have lunch waiting for me. I'd better get home. I'll be back later to check on the patient."

"Thank you, Doctor," Emily said.

Raider looked at Doc and scratched his head. "I know where I left that body, Doc, and I saw with my own two eyes that it's gone. Who the hell would want an old lady's dead body except the undertaker?"

"Beats me," Doc said, "but to be honest with you, Raider, it's not the most important thing on my mind right now."

"No, I suppose not. I'll go get the girls. You want to meet me later?"

"Sure. Come back here after dinner, and we'll go over the case in more detail."

Raider drove the wagon to the hotel and stepped into the lobby, where a group of Dead Rabbits was accosting the brides. One of them had his arms around Ann's waist and was saying, "I know your kind, honey. How about a little kiss for me?"

She brought her knee up into his groin, and he doubled over in pain. His friends laughed. He glared at her as he slowly straightened his body and said, "You shouldn't have done that, bitch."

"Why not?" Ann said. "I think I know your kind better than you know mine."

As he drew an open hand back to strike her, Raider grasped his wrist, his black eyes piercing deeply into the Irishman's. The room became deathly quiet.

"Where I come from," Raider said without breaking the stare, "it ain't nice to hit a lady."

"Where I come from," the Irishman said, "there ain't too many ladies."

The other Dead Rabbits laughed.

"Get your asses out of here," Raider said.

"Figure you can make us?"

"No doubt about it," Raider said, stepping back and dropping his hand to his holster.

The Irishman mumbled, "I'll leave, cowboy, but I won't forget."

He turned and then spun around and threw a wild punch at Raider's head. But Raider had been in too many scuffles to fall for such an old trick. He ducked under the errant punch and delivered a straight blow to the Irishman's abdomen, sending him sprawling to the ground and gasping for air.

"Next," Raider said to the other Dead Rabbits.

Two of them stepped forward, helped their friend to his feet, and then moved silently out of the hotel.

"Thanks for the help," Ann said. "I want to repay you."

"I'd like to take you up on that," Raider said, "but it's time for you girls to meet your new husband."

"Blimey," said Ann, "I suppose it is."

"What about Agnes?" Molly asked. "When is the funeral?" Two of the girls started to cry at the mention of her name.

"I'm making all the arrangements," Raider said, realizing that he didn't even know where her body was. "Just leave it to me."

"She was like me own mum," someone said.

"A good woman."

"A saint, she was."

When they were outside, Raider saw several of the Dead Rabbits gathered around Yankee Sullivan. He kept his eye on them as he loaded the girls into the wagon, and as they rolled past the gang, Raider looked down at the Rabbits' leader.

Once the wagon had passed, Sullivan turned to a cohort and asked, "You sure?"

"I seen it myself," he answered, "just before I left New York."

"My second in command is dead, and you didn't even tell me?"

"I only got into town an hour ago."

"Then I should have known an hour ago, you asshole. Are you positive?"

"Look, Yankee, Dick Jameson is dead, and that's the fellow who did it. I seen it with my own eyes."

"Well, stick around, then, because I promise you you'll see plenty more when that cowboy butts heads with me again."

CHAPTER FOURTEEN

Raider guided the wagon into a long, circular gravel driveway in front of Daniel Edmonds's spectacular mansion.

"I can't believe it," Ann said. "I've never seen anything so big, save for the Queen's palace."

Raider grabbed a few of their bags, and they went to the door, but before they could knock, it opened. A blue-haired old lady dressed in traditional maid's garb looked them up and down and then said, "Mr. Edmonds is expecting you."

"That so?" Raider said. "How'd he know we'd be here today?"

"He didn't," she said, straight-faced. "He's had me standing at this door every day for the past two weeks. Come in. Don't tarry."

They followed her through palatial halls and into a stunning, massive library. There, sitting in a large upholstered chair and reading a book, was Daniel Edmonds. He appeared to be about forty years old; brittle amber hair crowned a face filled with innocent bliss. Although he looked directly at his visitors, he seemed barely to notice them. Finally, he stood. His height was surprising, about six feet four inches, with his gangly body making him appear even taller.

"I'm Daniel Edmonds," he said.

Raider extended his hand and said, "Mr. Edmonds, my name is Raider. I escorted these ladies across the country. I know you're expecting a female guardian, but she—"

"A female guardian?"

"Yeah. I was told you wanted a female guardian to guarantee their virtue."

"Oh, yes, now I remember. Well, where is she?"

"She's dead, Mr. Edmonds."

"Oh, my gracious, how terrible."

"She was killed by Indians."

Edmonds face grew distant as he thought for a few seconds. "Well," he said, "if she's dead, she can't very well attest to anybody's virtue, can she?"

"No, she can't, but she was with the girls until just recently, and I'm sure she would have spoken highly of them."

Edmonds looked each girl over carefully. "They look virtuous enough to me," he said.

"That's it?" Raider said.

"That's it."

"Then I guess I'll be on my way."

"No, please, Mr. Raider, I wouldn't think of it. A man who travels across the country for me deserves a dinner at the very least. Please join us."

"Now that you mention it, I ain't had a scrap since breakfast."

Edmonds turned to the maid, "Hilda. Oh, have you people been properly introduced to Hilda?"

"No."

"Well, this is Hilda. I suppose that's proper enough." He laughed. "Hilda, there will be eight for dinner tonight."

"Fine, sir," she said. "It will be served shortly."

Raider and the brides followed Edmonds into the living room. He sat in a chair that looked more like a throne, and the girls and Raider scattered on chairs and sofas around him. He spread his arms as he spoke.

"So," he said, "welcome to—" Suddenly, his eyes closed and he was motionless. His guests looked at his face and then quizzically at each other.

"You'll have to understand," said Hilda as she entered the room. "Mr. Edmonds has narcolepsy."

"You mean he's dead?" Raider asked.

"No, he's not dead. Narcolepsy is a disease that causes Mr. Edmonds to fall asleep at odd times."

She dusted the table next to Edmonds as though nothing had happened. Raider and the girls didn't know what to do.

"So," Edmonds said, returning to consciousness, "how was your trip?"

"Fine," Raider said, too fascinated by the situation to go into any detail.

Hilda reentered the room and waved to Edmonds. "Looks like it's time for dinner," he said, waving back. "Shall we proceed to the dining room?"

In the center of the dining room was a huge, heavy carved-oak dining table. Around it were twelve spindleback chairs. There were eight solid-gold candlesticks on the table, and a crystal chandelier hung from the ceiling.

"Very impressive," said Raider.

"You haven't tasted anything yet, Mr. Raider."

"I meant your house," Raider said, laughing.

"Thank you."

"Do you mind if I ask what line of work you're in, Mr. Edmonds?"

"Huh?"

"I mean, how does a fellow end up with so much dough?"

"Oh, my money. My mother gave it to me."

"Sounds like you got quite a mother."

"She died."

"Sorry to hear it."

They sat at the table as Hilda served each course on a silver tray. Edmonds placidly eyed the roast turkey, cranberry sauce, and hot biscuits, but when a bowl of peas appeared in front of him, he leaped to his feet as though his pants had caught fire.

"What the hell is going on here!" he shouted.

"What's wrong?" Hilda asked as she scurried into the room.

"These peas."

"They tasted fine to me, Mr. Edmonds."

"I don't care about taste," he bellowed. "They're round!"

"So?" Raider asked. "I never seen a pea that wasn't."

"I despise putting anything round into my mouth. I positively hate things that roll around. It's like having bugs crawling all over my body. The mere thought of it makes me shiver. Take them away, now!"

"Yes, Mr. Edmonds," Hilda said.

Edmonds calmed down and returned to his seat. "I hope you ladies remember that," he said. "If not . . ." His narcolepsy struck, and he was asleep.

The girls and Raider looked at each other and fought to contain laughter that threatened to erupt at any moment.

Minutes later, Edmonds awoke and said, "Let's eat."

As Edmonds carved the turkey, Ann spoke up. "Aren't you interested in knowing anything about us, even our names?"

"Your names? There's really no need. I'll learn them all at the wedding."

"Wedding?"

"Weddings, actually. Dark or light meat?"

"When will the wedding . . . weddings take place?"

"As soon as we finish supper."

"Can't it wait until morning?" Raider asked.

"There's no need. I had one of my rooms converted into a chapel for the occasion. By the way, Mr. Raider, if you're not in a rush, perhaps you'd agree to be my best man."

Raider was dumbfounded by his host's behavior. He nodded and glanced nervously at the girls.

An hour later, the ceremony took place. A young Aaronic priest, who'd been staying with Edmonds for the last month so that he'd always be on tap, conducted it. One by one, the girls cautiously stepped up to Edmonds and the priest pronounced the vows proclaiming them man and wife. Twenty minutes later, Daniel Edmonds had six new wives.

CHAPTER FIFTEEN

"Okay, now for Dave Mather."

"Why do we have to do this, Doc? I don't care where these guys are from or what their goddamn modus operandi is."

"We have to do it, Raider, because Pinkerton says we have to do it. Besides, it might save your life if you know who you're up against."

"Shit, Doc, I still say it's a waste of time. It's boring."

"And you're the most pigheaded bastard I ever knew. The faster you do it, the faster you'll get out of here." Raider sulked. "Now what do you know about Mather?"

"I know he's an outlaw. Dodge City, I think."

"That's right. They call him Mysterious Dave because he doesn't speak much. Some folks say he only talks to tell a man he's going to kill him."

"Does he?"

"Every time."

"I'll listen close to the man."

"Anyway, I know he's here. I've seen him up at the bishop's."

"Who's next."

"John Wesley Hardin."

"I know about him. He's dangerous company."

"Ever met him?"

"Nope."

"I did this week. He's taken a liking to me, and I'm a little uncomfortable with it."

"How's that?"

"Just a hunch. I don't think he's got all his bread in the oven, if you know what I mean. He might explode at any minute."

"A sick son of a bitch is what I hear," Raider said.

"That's what I meant when I said . . . forget it. I guess that's everybody except the Dead Rabbits, but there's no way a country boy like you would know anything about them."

"Dead Rabbits gang?"

"Yeah."

"So they were heading for Utah, after all."

"What are you talking about?"

"I met me a Dead Rabbit while I was playing cards in New York, only he's a lot deader now than when I met him."

"You killed him?"

"He tried to shoot me in the back."

"Do you know his name?"

"Jameson, I think."

"Dick Jameson?"

"That's the guy."

"Christ, Raider, he's their next to the top man."

"What are you getting so worked up about? It ain't the first time we've shot an outlaw."

"The Dead Rabbits have a reputation to protect. They always seek revenge when somebody kills one of their own, and some say they always get it."

"Is that so?" Raider said. "I got me a reputation of my own."

"Nobody can shoot or fight like you, Raider, and nobody knows it better than I. But the odds are against us this time. There's lots of them and only two of us, so let's keep a low profile, okay?"

"If you say so, only . . ."

"You haven't gotten into trouble already, have you?"

Raider thought briefly of his confrontation with the Dead Rabbits in the hotel lobby, looked at Doc innocently, and said, "Hell, no, I've only been here a few hours."

"Good."

"Are we finished? I want to get some sleep."

"Almost."

"What's left to do?"

"We have to contact Wagner."

"Forget it."

"Raider."

"I said forget it. I ain't climbing any poles. I'm bushed. Besides, you've been sitting around Salt Lake City all this time having fun while I damn near got killed a dozen times. You climb the fucking pole."

"We've been through this a thousand times," Doc said as he removed a telegraph lever and trunnions from a drawer. "We're partners because our skills complement each other, and one of your skills happens to be climbing poles."

"Well, I never should have told you about that one," Raider said, obviously relenting.

"Just do it. Then you can go to bed."

"Don't talk to me, Doc. Give me the fucking equipment, but don't say one word."

"Atta boy, Partner."

Raider grabbed the equipment and went outside. He returned in ten minutes.

"What did Wagner say?" asked Doc.

"You know I don't read any dumb-ass code."

"That's right, I forgot. It's not one of your skills."

"Don't push me, Doc."

Before deciphering the message Raider had scrawled, Doc removed an Old Virginia cheroot from his breast pocket and put it in his mouth. He reached for a match, but Raider snared the cheroot from Doc's lips and broke it in half.

"Damn it, Raider, what the hell did you do that for?"

"I hate those stinking cheroots."

"They help me relax."

"And they make me sick, and it just so happens that one of my skills is beating the shit out of guys who make me sick."

Doc knew that he was licked and turned his attention to the message. "God almighty," he said after decoding it, "it's even worse than I thought. I sent some bullets to Chicago from the last Indian attack to have them checked. Wagner says they come out of some mighty fancy weapons."

"So?"

"It just seems strange to me that these outlaws would be selling such fancy pieces."

Before Raider could answer, there was a knock at the door.

"Who's that?" Doc asked.

"How the hell do you expect me to know without opening the door?"

"Did anybody see you sending that message?"

"Hell, no."

"You sure?"

"Of course I'm sure. It's another of my skills."

"Open it slowly."

Doc drew his gun and stood to the side as Raider pulled the door open. It was Emily Stover.

"It's you," said Doc.

"Who were you expecting? You told me to stop by later."

"That's right. I forgot."

"I saw something that might interest you, Doc."

"What's that?"

"Three men just came riding through town with a whole bunch of folks chasing after them like they were famous or something. They headed up the road toward the bishop's place."

"Three men?" said Raider. "What'd they look like?"

"They were nice enough looking, early thirties, I'd say. They wore long riding coats and rode fancy horses."

"That's it?" asked Doc.

"There is one other thing."

"Oh?"

"One of them waved to the crowd. I may be wrong, but I think he was missing a finger."

Raider and Doc turned to each other and at the same instant said, "Jesse James."

"Oh, my goodness," Emily said, her fingers to her lips and her eyes open wide.

CHAPTER SIXTEEN

Raider sopped up excess maple syrup on his plate with the last of his pancakes and shoved it in his mouth. He grunted his approval and wiped his moustache with the back of his hand.

"I'm glad to see you liked my breakfast, Mr. Raider," Emily said, beaming.

"I certainly do, ma'am. There ain't nothing better than buckwheat pancakes to get the morning started. My mama used to make me buckwheat cakes darn near every morning."

"Sounds like you had a good mother."

"Yes, ma'am, I surely did."

"Listen," Doc said, interrupting. "I'd love to sit around and praise Raider's mother, but we have work to do."

"Yeah, I figured that," Raider said. "You're fattening me up for something, and you might as well tell me what it is."

"I want you to go in there, Raider."

"In where?"

"The bishop's. Jesse James is the most famous outlaw in this country, and I don't have to tell you how much Pinkerton wants him."

"You sure don't."

"We can't sit here and do nothing. Besides, I have a feeling that whatever they've been planning is about to come off. If they were waiting on anybody, it would be James."

"All well and good, but I just can't waltz into the bishop's place."

"I've got it worked out. Does the name Matt Pike ring a bell?"

"I've heard of him. Why?"

"As far as the bishop's friends are concerned, you are now Matt Pike."

"I don't follow. What if some of these boys know Pike?"

"There is no Pike."

"That's crazy."

"Pinkerton invented him for undercover assignments. They put his name on their wanted list, even put up posters advertising a reward."

"No shit? That's pretty dang smart of them."

"Coming from you, that's a real compliment." Doc took out a cheroot and held it up for inspection.

"Would you put that goddamn thing away," Raider said.

Doc ignored him, held the cheroot an inch from his nose, and gently sniffed. "What a delightful aroma," he said.

"I'm warning you, Doc, you're getting on my nerves. Christ, I think I'd rather spend my time with Jesse James than a pain in the butt like you."

Doc lit the Old Virginia, inhaled, and then released a few small puffs of smoke. "Be that as it may, Raider, you can't just rush in there without knowing what you're doing. What do you know about Jesse James?"

Raider frowned. "Let's see. He comes from Missouri,

likes to ride with his brother, the Youngers, Clell Miller, and a few other boys. What else should I know?"

"Enough to give you the advantage and to keep you alive, although I don't know why I bother caring." He took a notebook from his pocket. "I'll read you notes from my journal. 'James, Jesse Woodson. Born 1847 in Clay County, Missouri. Five feet eleven inches, muscular, blue eyes, brown hair, missing most of middle finger on left hand. Married, wife's name Zerelda . . . two kids . . . original occupation, farmer. Wanted for innumerable counts of murder, bank robbery, train robbery. Reward, $20,000.' "

Doc put down the notebook and looked at his Pinkerton partner. "He's smart, Raider, as smart as they come. He's not fast, can't touch you for speed, but they say he's a crack shot. Give him time to shoot, and he'll hit just about anything. And remember, James isn't the only gunslinger to worry about up there. One is crazier than the next."

"When do you want me to go?"

"The sooner the better."

"I'll run back to the hotel and grab a few things, then ride up there."

"Aren't you forgetting something?"

Raider shrugged.

"Who is Matt Pike?"

"I thought you said it was some name Pinkerton made up."

"That's right, but you have to know the background that goes with him. What if these boys start asking you questions?"

"All right, let's hear it."

"Pike's supposed to be from the Southwest, Arkansas and Texas."

"I can handle that."

"Mostly a bank robber, plus a few stagecoaches and a gunfighter. The reward is $5,000."

"You mean Jesse James is worth more than me?"

Doc grinned. "Afraid so."

There was a knock at the door. Emily answered it and then returned to the kitchen and said, "Doc, there's a kid at the door sent over by Hastings. He says that Frenchman you brought in is conscious, and he thinks you should come over right away to talk to him. It doesn't look like he'll last too much longer."

"All right, I'll be right over." Doc stood and adjusted his tie. "Be careful, Raider, and let me make the decisions. Don't try to contact me. I'll see you there and in town."

"Okay."

"I have to go now. Good luck."

Doc left and Raider finished his coffee, said good-bye to Emily, and went to the hotel. A few minutes later, he was on the road and heading for the bishop's, wearing a .44 on each hip and carrying a 30-30. He reached the house and dismounted.

"You don't look like a Mormon to me," a voice from behind him said.

Raider turned and looked into a face that needed no introduction. "No, I'm not," he said. "I heard this might be a good place for a fellow like me to stay a spell, maybe even make a couple of bucks."

"Could be. What did you say your name was?"

"I didn't, but it's Pike, Matt Pike."

"So you're Pike. I've heard good things about you. I'm Jesse James."

"I know."

The two men shook hands, and Raider made sure to squeeze a little harder than usual.

"Come on inside, Pike," James said. "I'll introduce you around and buy you a drink."

"Don't mind if I do."

They walked through the main entrance and entered a large barroom where there were card tables, a stage, and every amusement ever invented.

"Quite a place," Raider said.

"Damn right. I couldn't believe it myself."

They were making their way between tables toward the stage when Yankee Sullivan pushed his chair into their path.

"How come you're walking between tables instead of around them?" he asked.

"How come you don't mind your own fucking business?" Raider said, staring coldly at the Dead Rabbits' leader.

"Dick Jameson is my business, mister."

"Jameson?"

"You remember Jameson from New York, you bastard."

"The name is Pike, Matt Pike, and if you don't move, you're likely to wear that chair as a permanent fixture on your ass."

Sullivan looked at Raider and James, smirked, and pulled his chair in. Raider took in who was with him. Then he accompanied James to the bar.

"Old friend of yours?" James asked with a devilish grin.

"Never seen him before, but apparently I met one of his friends."

"Sounds more like an ex-friend."

"He drew a fifth ace."

"That'll do it every time."

"Amen."

The barmaid, an attractive seventeen-year-old blond, asked, "What will it be, Mr. James?"

"Call me Jesse, and it'll be bourbon." He looked at Raider, who nodded and said, "Make that two." The drinks were served, and both men gulped them down.

"So," said James, "I thought that Irish prick said you did your deed in New York."

"That's right."

"I heard you worked around Arkansas."

"I do, but I wasn't in New York working, just visiting friends."

James' brother and Cole Younger entered the barroom and stood by the door.

"Listen, Pike, I have some business to attend to," James said. "Why don't you order us another round, and I'll be back in a minute."

Raider ordered two more bourbons and sat at a table. He saw Sullivan and the Dead Rabbits looking at him and talking among themselves. Then a tall, young, thickly muscled man got up, sauntered over to Raider, stood over him, and grinned.

"You got a problem?" Raider asked without looking up.

"You're Pike?"

"Yup."

"I've been looking for you for a long time. I'm Kid Cummings."

Raider now looked up at the eighteen-year-old gunslinger. The word out of east Texas was that he was one of the fastest draws around.

"Well," said Raider, "looks like you found me."

"People say you're fast, Pike."

"People who know how fast I am are all dead."

"People say you're from Arkansas."

"So?"

"So I'm from Arkansas, too. It ain't such a big place."

"Listen, kid, you're too young for this shit. I'd kill you, only your mother would get upset. Beat it."

"Make me, Pike."

Raider picked up his glass, brought it to his lips, and

swallowed. He stood, brushed off his pants, and said, "Let's go."

A buzz swept through the room. Rowdy Joe Lowe jumped up on a table and yelled, "Hold it right there!" Everyone looked at him. "You boys are going to have to settle your differences right inside here. We can't be killing each other out in front of the bishop's. Besides, we could all use a little entertainment." The crowd cheered.

Lowe stepped between the men, a silver dollar in his hand. "I'm going to throw this here coin up in the air," he said. "When it hits the ground, and not before, you can start shootin'."

Cummings' eyes shot back and forth between Raider and Lowe, but Raider's eyes never left his adversary. Tension in the room swelled. Then Lowe giggled and flipped the coin high into the air. The first sound was that of the coin hitting the wood floor. Instantly, a shot followed, and Kid Cummings dropped to the ground, a bullet through his heart; his gun never cleared its holster.

Raider walked slowly back to his table and sat down.

"Not bad," said Jesse James. "Here's your drink."

"Thanks," said Raider, downing the bourbon.

"You figure that was the smartest thing to do?" James asked.

"It was the only thing to do."

"Just be careful, Pike. There are a lot of swelled heads in this room. Everybody wants to prove they're faster than the next slob, and they don't always play fair."

"I'll just have to be on my guard, then." Raider said.

The orgy started an hour later. There were enough prostitutes in the barroom to serve approximately a hundred and twenty men. Raider made his way to the bar but couldn't find the barmaid. He stepped behind it to pour his own drink, looked down, and grinned. The young barmaid was in a sixty-nine position on the floor with Jesse James. Raider stepped over them, grabbed an entire bottle of bourbon, opened it, sat down at a table, and watched the show. His own sex life had been a little less active than usual, but he decided to sit this one out. When it came to sex, he preferred the basic approach: one-on-one straight-ahead screwing.

He sipped from the bottle and looked around the room. Rowdy Joe Lowe, a giant gunfighter with a handlebar moustache, was naked on a table in the center of the room with three women. One of them wore nothing but his stovepipe hat, another teased him with his own gun, and he drunkenly pawed at the third.

Johnny Ringo was screwing a girl who couldn't have been more than twelve, and Billie Clanton had hog-tied a wrinkled, middle-aged whore. The scene was ludicrous to Raider, and he laughed loudly.

John Wesley Hardin watched without emotion. Dave Mather was in another corner, reading a book. Raider knew from Doc that these men were the ones he should worry about most. They were there for business, and that business meant killing anybody who got in their way.

Raider had seen enough. He picked up his bottle and headed for his room. As he walked down the long corridor, he was confronted by a young whore, about nineteen in his judgment.

"Hello there, little lady," he said, beginning to reconsider his stand on abstinence.

"Hi." She had long curly red hair and wore nothing but a pale green cotton teddy.

"What's a fine-looking young woman like you doing in a place like this?"

She laughed nervously and said, "I was beginning to wonder that myself. I don't come from around here. I live up in Oregon, and I'm getting a lot of money to do this, but I've never seen so many crazy men in my life. Where I come from, all everyone wants to do is fuck. Here, they're all sort of . . . well, sick.''

Raider's eyes moved deliberately up and down her frame. She was fair-skinned, with an occasional freckle highlighting her shoulders and arms. Her breasts pressed tight against the teddy. Her soft, white legs looked more like a schoolgirl's than a prostitute's.

"We're not all sick," he said. "Some of us still like to fuck.''

Her smile was as wide as a river as she purred. "Lead the way.''

Raider's room was in a remote corner of the bishop's mansion. They walked arm in arm down the narrow hall. Raider dropped his hand to her ass, and she giggled.

"It's not too much further," he said.

They entered the small room, and the girl went straight for a candle and lit it.

"What are you doing that for?'' Raider asked.

"I like to see what I'm doing. Besides, it's my name.''

"Your name?''

"That's right, my name is Fire.''

Raider laughed. "Somehow I can't see a proud mama looking at her beautiful little girl and calling her Fire.''

"Can you see her calling me Beulah?''

"No.''

"Me, neither. That's why it's Fire.''

Raider didn't understand her reasoning but wasn't about to argue.

She stood in the glow of the candle and dropped the teddy to the floor. She was slighter than Raider had imagined, with the bones in her shoulders and ribs easily visible. But her breasts were large and round, and the milky skin of her upper thighs was as white as the finest marble.

"I think it's time to put out my fire," she said, going to him. She unbuttoned his shirt, and he cupped her bare ass. "No," she said, "wait. We have all night." She removed his shirt and brushed her breasts against his skin. Her tongue made gentle circles over his nipples as she undid his denims. He reached for her breasts, but again she said, "No, not yet."

Soon they were both naked, and Raider's cock was as hard as it would ever be. She lay on the bed, looked up at him and mouthed a kiss, spread her legs wide, and whispered, "It's time."

He knelt next to her and ran his hand along her soft thigh.

"There's no need for that," she said. "I'm ready, and I see you are, too."

He resisted and began kissing her nipple.

"Please," she said, "there's only one thing I like, and that's fucking. I like it so much. Please."

Raider obliged and rammed the old avenger home. Within seconds she was moaning, writhing, and clawing at his back.

"More," she screamed, "do it more, deeper and harder."

Raider increased the rhythm until he finally released in a pulsating orgasm.

He looked down at where perspiration had caused her hair to mat across her forehead. She breathed deeply and had a pained expression on her face.

"Did I hurt you?" he asked.

"I need more," she panted. "I need it so badly."

She took his flaccid organ in her hand and vigorously stroked it. Then she drew it close to the well-lubricated lips of her vulva and ran it up and down. As soon as it began to stir, she tried to force it inside. She had the look of an animal in heat, and Raider was to eager to satisfy her.

His penis came back to full life as he mounted her for another round. He moved in and out at a feverish pace, with her legs wrapped around him so tightly that he was only able to withdraw slightly.

"Harder," she screamed. "Slam it into me. I love it."

His legs were beginning to cramp, but he continued to heed her nymphomaniacal orders. Her grip around his waist tightened, and the sound of their bellies slapping together grew louder.

"Jesus Christ," she gasped, "please don't stop, oh, please, please don't stop."

She was now so out of control that he had to hold her tight just to keep her beneath him. He slammed into her harder, trying to satiate her incredible sexual appetite, until they came together in a mutual volcanic eruption.

Raider couldn't remember ever having been so satisfied. He rolled off and looked at her. She was soaked with sweat, her hair a series of wet red strings. There was a swelling near her vagina and red blotches on much of her skin. She smiled up at him.

"That was mighty nice, little lady," he said. "I promise you I'll remember it for a long time."

"What do you mean *was*?" she said indignantly. "I thought you said you liked fucking."

"I sure do, but I figured we were through for the night."

She purred as she took his limp penis in her mouth, saying, "You must think they call me Fire because of my red hair. The fire's inside, big boy, *deep* inside."

His erection returned. He took her in his arms and said, "Well, little lady, let's see if we can put that fire out tonight."

CHAPTER SEVENTEEN

"Dr. Weatherbee, I'm so glad to see you again. Won't you please come in?"

Doc stepped into Bishop Lee's office and sat across the desk from his host. "It's nice to see you again, too, sir," he said.

"Tell me, Doctor, have you decided that the Church of the Latter Day Saints is the best way for you, after all?"

"I haven't made up my mind yet, Bishop. To be honest, it's not religion that brings me here today."

"Oh, what is it?"

Doc put a cheroot in his mouth and offered one to the bishop.

"No thank you, Doctor, we value moderation."

"Oh, I'm sorry," said Doc, putting it away.

"Don't be silly. This is my home, and I want my guests to be comfortable. Please smoke."

Doc lit the cheroot and said, "I suppose you heard that a second wagon train was hit by Indians just north of here."

"Yes, I did hear that. Unfortunate."

"Well, this one was quite a bit worse than the last one. The only survivor was a little boy."

"I'd heard there was one other survivor."

"The boy's father died this morning."

"Were you able to learn anything from him?"

"No, I'm afraid not."

"What a shame."

"Do you mind if I stand, sir?" Doc asked.

"If you wish."

He inhaled his cheroot and took a few steps toward the window. "This is a difficult thing to say to such a respected and well-meaning man as yourself, sir."

"Please, Doctor, don't mince words. What is it you wish to say?"

"Well, I have reason to believe that the men you entertain here have organized a massive gun-selling ring that's given the Indians the ability to destroy wagon trains heading west."

"Reason to believe, Doctor? My religion frowns on speculation and false witness."

"I pulled shells from those Frenchmen, sir. The Indians were using fancy pistols, no doubt about that. I figure the only place they could have gotten them is from the boys holed up here. Certainly, none of your God-fearing followers in town would be responsible."

Lee frowned and said in measured tones, "I know this territory as well as anyone. I've been here a long time and have seen a lot happen. I know that what you're saying could very well be true, but I also know that I've chosen to follow the ways of the Lord. Those ways do not allow me to close my doors to these men because they might have done something wrong in the past. I would be lax in my duty if I did not give them the benefit of the doubt." He smiled. "But I'd also be lax in my duty if I didn't try to learn the truth of this matter, and you have my word as a member of the cloth that I'll do just that.''

"I can't ask for more," Doc said. "We may save a lot of lives in the bargain."

The two men shook hands, and Doc left the office just as John Wesley Hardin came up the hall.

"Good morning," Doc said. "How are you?"

"Like a million bucks, Doc, like a million."

The gunfighter continued past him and into the bishop's office without knocking. Doc stared at the door a moment and then continued on. Farther down the hall stood Raider.

"Hello, Doc," said the big man.

"Mr. Pike." They both checked that they were not being observed. "Well, what's it like?" Doc asked.

"You wouldn't believe it. This place is the biggest brothel in the West."

"What are you talking about?"

"There were dozens of whores here last night. They had the biggest party I ever did see, and none of it cost anybody a cent."

"What do these guys do all day?"

"Nothing. They drink, play cards, bang whores, fight, but never work. It's like some kind of vacation home for gunslingers."

"Did you see James?"

"I drank with him yesterday. He kind of took a liking to me."

"Why?"

"I guess you might say I got into a little altercation."

"How little?"

"I killed Kid Cummings."

"You don't know when to stop, do you?"

"I had no choice."

Two men approached them, and they stopped talking. After they'd passed, Doc said, "Just be careful, Raider.

I'm sure there's a lot of competition with these guys, and a lot of them are damn good.''

"You're right there, Doc, and you were right about Hardin. I'm not sure he's got it all upstairs.''

The bishop's door opened, and Hardin emerged. The two Pinkertons were silent as he slowly moved past them, his glazed eyes looking straight ahead. He passed without a word as if he hadn't seen either of them.

Doc asked Raider, "Is there anything else I should know before I leave?''

"One thing. I saw Emily's neighbor here.''

"Schwartze?''

"If that's his name. He was here all day. If I was you Doc, I'd find out who he really is.''

"Okay, I will. Remember, Raider, this place is danger-ous, explosive. The bishop doesn't know which end is up, thinks he's saving souls. If things get too hot, get out. We'll let it cool and come back.''

"That doesn't sound like Doc Weatherbee.''

"I'm serious, Raider. We've never dealt with anything like this.''

"Okay, I'm with you.''

Although it was almost noon, Raider had been awake only a short time. His night with Fire had left him ex-hausted. He went into the barroom for a cup of coffee. Seated at a table in the corner were Jesse James, Frank James, and Cole Younger. Jesse saw Raider and called him over. Raider took his coffee and headed for the outlaws.

"Good morning,'' said Jesse. "That was a hell of a party last night, huh?''

"Sure enough.''

"I'd like you to meet my brother, Frank, and my old friend and business partner, Cole Younger.''

Frank was as handsome as Jesse; he had the same blue

eyes and sensuous mouth but was bigger and possessed a squarer jaw. Younger was wiry and more weather-beaten in his appearance than the James brothers.

"Sit down, Pike," said Jesse.

Raider sat and sipped from his cup.

Cole Younger looked up and said, "You're pretty good."

"Beg your pardon."

"I saw you with Cummings."

"Just doing what had to be done."

"Ain't that the truth."

"What Cole's trying to say," said Jesse, "is that we could use a man like you in our business."

"I like working alone."

"The James gang made $60,000 last year, Pike. You ain't making that kind of money down in Arkansas."

"I do just fine as it is."

"We got a big job in mind, Pike, and a reason we come all the way out here is to find the best guns around. Not just good guns, the best. Some said it was Cummings, but you proved different."

"It could be a one-time thing," Frank James said. "Your take might be twenty grand."

"Word's out that you fellows are real hot. Pinkerton is after you."

"Old man Pinkerton gives us a spot of trouble now and then, but not as much as we give him." They laughed loudly. "I think Allan Pinkerton finally learned to stay away from me," Jesse said.

"Well, I'll think about it," Raider said. "What else can you tell me?"

"Just that it's a train, it's loaded, and we need a fast gun. That's about it for now."

"When do I have to let you know?"

"The job comes up Friday. It's the last one for these

parts. After that, we're heading for Missouri. You can come with us or you can stay here.''

"I'll let you know."

Raider finished his coffee and put the cup down on the table. "Gentlemen," he said, "I think I'll sleep off last night's party, if you don't mind. See you later."

CHAPTER EIGHTEEN

Emily Stover had been awake for nearly an hour. She lay quietly next to Doc and stroked his thick bicep with her fingers. He awoke and took a moment to get his bearings.

"Emily," he asked, "what time is it?"

"I guess about eight o'clock."

"How come you're not asleep?"

"I've been laying here thinking."

"Something wrong?"

"No, just thinking about how nice it is to have a man next to me when I wake up in the morning. I'd nearly forgotten, Doc. It's so good, it takes my breath away."

"I feel the same way."

"I'm going to miss you, Doc, when you move on."

"I'll miss you, too."

"You'll find somebody else."

"So will you."

"I don't know. Maybe, maybe not. You've taught me a lot about myself."

"I hope I've convinced you what a beautiful woman you are."

"You're sweet."

Doc turned and faced her. "I'm not gone yet," he said. "There's no reason to miss me so soon."

He kissed her lightly on the nose, and she laughed. He found her lips and plunged his tongue deep into her mouth, probing every crevice as he pulled her body closer to his.

He removed her blue silk nightgown, and her naked body suddenly became very hot. His index finger flicked at her erect nipples as she straddled his hips and pressed her wet, warm pubis against his still penis. He reached behind her and placed his hands under her ass and then guided her forward until her vulva dangled inches from his mouth. He craned his neck and gently kissed the triangular patch of flaxed hair. He repeated the kiss before licking her clitoris.

"God." She gasped. "I can't tell you how good that feels."

He curled his tongue and plunged it as deeply as he could into her vagina; then he withdrew it and toyed with the clitoris again.

"Don't stop," she moaned.

He continued licking until her legs went into spasm and her lips pressed tightly together to suppress gasps of pleasure. As she came, she pressed her cunt so hard against his face that he couldn't breathe.

"That was nice," she said as they languished together in the afterglow of her sexual pleasure.

They were both silent for a moment.

"Do you ever think about Clint, Doc?"

"Sure."

"I mean when you're with me. Do you wonder what he would think if he knew we were doing this?"

"I guess it's crossed my mind."

"I really don't think he'd mind. If you did it while he was alive, he would have killed you, partner or not. But he's dead, and I have a feeling he'd think of me first, like he always did.''

"I hope so.''

She looked down at his still rock-hard erection. ''Look at that,'' she said ''We'd better do something about it.''

"What do you have in mind?''

"Like I said before, Doc, if I'm going to miss you, I'd better make sure I have plenty to miss.'' She took his cock in both hands and gently massaged it.

"Delightful,'' Doc said.

She climbed on top of him and kissed him hard. He caressed her breasts and then rolled her over on her back. Suddenly, he slid his hands beneath her and lifted her into his arms. They stood for a moment; she kissed his neck while her dangling right hand found his erection. He walked slowly across the room and set her down on an oak armoire. She looked up at him in wonderment. Now she understood what he intended. She spread her legs, which placed her at the perfect height to allow him to slide inside. She screamed with delight.

"Oh, Doc, I absolutely love it. This is—''

"Quiet. Save your breath.''

He pumped in and out with his hands against the wall for support. It didn't take long before her orgasm grabbed at his erection.

"Let's not stop,'' she said.

"I wouldn't think of it.''

She wrapped her legs tightly around him and wiggled her hips and within minutes, Doc exploded inside her.

"Oh God, Doc, I am going to miss this.''

They had breakfast in the kitchen.

"Delicious,'' Doc said as he feasted on bacon and eggs. "Sex always makes me hungry.''

She filled her own plate and sat across from him. "How's Raider?'' she asked.

"He seemed okay yesterday, only he got into some trouble."

"What sort of trouble?"

"A gunfight with a punk slinger named Cummings."

"Raider killed him?"

"Yeah. I never have to worry about Raider. He can always handle himself.

"I remember when you were the wild one and Clint kept putting a tether on you to keep you from getting your head blown off."

"I got smart eventually."

They finished breakfast, and Emily cleared the table. "Doc," she said, "I'd like you to help me with something this morning."

"Just name it."

"Hearing you and Raider talk has reminded me how much I really hate all this spy stuff. I'd appreciate it if you'd help me straighten out Clint's study, you know, put things in order."

"Of course, Emily, I'd be happy to."

He took her by the elbow and escorted her into the study.

She laughed nervously as she said, "I don't know where to start."

"Start where ever you like and take your time."

She walked to the corner and opened a burlap bag that held many of Clint's mementos. She removed them one by one; guns and ammunition, receipts from hotels all over the West, and hundreds of seemingly meaningless pieces of paper.

"Didn't you throw away anything?" Doc asked.

"I guess not. This is the first time I ever opened this bag." She removed a horseshoe. "Remember Belle?"

"Sure do, the prettiest filly I ever saw. There were times I wondered if he'd trade you for that critter."

"He still had her when we moved up to Oregon, and when she died, he pulled this horseshoe off her foot. I guess he figured it would bring him more luck than it brought her. Truth is, Doc, it didn't do much good for either of them." She brushed away a tear and said, "I'm sorry."

"Don't be, Emily. He meant a heck of a lot to me, too."

"I know."

She pulled a small box from the sack and said, "This one is for you."

"Cheroots." He laughed. "God, he was even worse than me. Don't ever let Raider know he got me started on these things or he'll probably never speak to you again."

"Personally," she said, a smile in her voice, "I'm on Raider's side."

She pulled out tintypes and menus from restaurants in which he and Doc had eaten. There were also a dozen wanted posters of men they'd apprehended. By the time the bag was empty, Doc was flooded with memories.

"I wonder why I saved all this," Emily mused. "It probably means more to you than to me."

"Maybe, maybe not."

They turned their attention to the desk. Doc picked up the case journal. "Lots here," he said. "He took good notes."

"Take your time."

"I don't even want to start. I wouldn't be able to put it down." He started to close the book and then stopped. "Emily, what's this?"

"What?"

"These entries from Oregon and from Salt Lake City."

"I don't know. Clint kept writing in his journal even after he left Pinkerton."

"Listen to this. 'Another wagon train of Frenchmen

arrived at the logging plant today. Twelve of them had been killed near Salt Lake. Same location as the last three. Say it was Indians. Not a tribe I ever heard of.' ''

"Are you saying Clint knew about this and that's why he came to Utah?"

"Could be, if I know Clint."

Doc turned a couple of pages and read aloud: '' 'Met Lee today. Told him I wanted to be a Mormon. There is no longer any doubt, Bishop John Lee was responsible for Mountain Meadows.' ''

"For what?"

"Mountain Meadows massacre. A wagon train was knocked off at Mountain Meadows near here by Indians. The folks surrendered, threw down their guns, but the Indians shot them anyway, killed every one of them, over a hundred and fifty people."

"And Clint thought Bishop Lee was somehow responsible?"

"It sounds to me like he was sure of it."

"What does it mean?"

"For one thing, it may answer a lot of questions about why your husband's death was so mysterious."

"You don't think . . ."

"Maybe he was killed by Lee. Clint Stover wouldn't have made a mistake this big in a case. Maybe he got the goods on Lee, and Lee took care of him."

"That's unbelievable. What are you going to do?"

"I'll promise you one thing, Emily. If John Lee killed Clint, he'll hang for it. But I'm afraid that's going to have to wait right now."

"Why?"

"Because if Lee killed Clint for being suspicious of him, he won't hesitate to kill Raider, and he's got just the right houseguests up there to do it in a big way."

CHAPTER NINETEEN

"Mr. Pike, the bishop wants to see you in his office right away."

Raider looked through sleepy eyes at the young Aaronic priest standing in the doorway of his bedroom. "All right," he muttered, "I'll be there in a couple of minutes."

The priest disappeared, and Raider tried to rub the sleep from his eyes. He stood, clasped his hands together behind his back, and tried to stretch his weary back muscles. The socks he picked up off the floor had a hole in them, and so he went to his bureau and removed a fresh pair. He pulled a pair of denims over his shorts, scratched his chest a few times, and then put on an old cotton undershirt he'd hung on the bedpost. The bishop? he thought to himself. What the hell does the bishop want with me?

He checked his pocket watch. Eight-thirty, early for the bishop's place. He was probably the only one up. He confirmed it as he walked down the long empty corridor leading to the bishop's office. He was still in his stocking feet, and his footsteps were silent.

The big oak office door was slightly ajar. Raider prepared to knock, when the bishop's hearty voice said,

"Come on in." Raider slowly stepped inside and looked around. "Mr. Pike, I hope I didn't wake you. I've been up working for nearly three hours. Sometimes I forget that everybody else sleeps till nine or ten."

"There isn't much else to do around here," Raider said.

"That's why we're here, Mr. Pike, so fellows like you can enjoy a chance to relax, sleep late, have fun without having to worry about the law. You are enjoying yourself, Mr. Pike, aren't you?"

"Yes, indeed, sir, I certainly am."

"Good. The whole reason I started this little vacation home is so that men like you, who've chosen to live a certain unusual life-style, can have a chance to enjoy life like the rest of us."

"That's mighty nice of you."

He smiled. "Actually, Mr. Pike, this little business does have its rewards as well."

"Oh?"

"I presume you've heard about the small jobs we arrange every couple of weeks."

Raider nodded. "Yup, I have, but I would like to hear more. I believe in doing things right if you're going to do them at all."

"My philosophy exactly, Mr. Pike."

"How about starting from the beginning?"

"Very well. The beginning was almost twenty years ago. It was just myself and some local boys, and I remember the first wagon train we hit. It was filled with old ladies, and all we got was a crate full of size 16 dresses." He laughed, and Raider joined him. "Obviously, things got better. For twenty years we hit about one a month and made a nice living for ourselves."

"But?" said Raider in anticipation.

"But we got sloppy. More and more wagon trains realized what was going on, and we had to start killing to protect ourselves. That was when our little philosophy came into play, Mr. Pike.''

"How's that?"

"If you're going to do it at all, do it right. I figured, who better to work with than men like you. That's when I started giving the best damn free vacations imaginable, all the women and booze you can handle in exchange for . . .''

"For hitting one lousy wagon train while we're enjoying your hospitality.''

"It's a fair exchange, wouldn't you say?''

"I sure would," Raider said softly. The pieces finally were fitting together in his mind.

"Try to enjoy your day as much as possible, because I'm afraid tomorrow is a work day. There's a big wagon train heading for California that'll pass south of here early in the morning. We'll be there by sunup.''

"What exactly will I be doing?''

"I've heard a lot of good things about you, Mr. Pike. You should prove to be very valuable. Our operation is simple. Three-quarters of the boys rush the wagon train, make a lot of noise, and cause a diversion. The others are strategically placed around the area to take care of anybody trying to run away. I understand you're something of a crack shot. Naturally, you'll be stationed on a ridge. I know you're new, Mr. Pike, so I'll tell you right now. *I don't like survivors.''*

"I understand," Raider said, remaining expressionless.

"Very well, then, I'll see you bright and early tomorrow.''

Raider returned to his room and lay on the bed, with his head propped against the wall. He was about to doze off, when Jesse James appeared in the doorway.

"You got the news?" he asked.

"Yup.''

"The bishop had me in his office last night going over the whole damn thing. I got to hand it to him. He's got this whole thing organized better than I ever figured he could with this mob.''

"Right you are," said Raider. "He had me in there at eight-thirty this morning."

"I didn't know how lucky I was." James laughed. He sat on the edge of the bed and asked, "Well, what do you think of this whole thing? Think he'll get away with it?"

Raider had built up such an animosity toward James over the years that their sudden friendship made him uncomfortable. The truth was that he found James to be straightforward and likable. He had to remind himself of the outlaw's deeds to keep himself from becoming too friendly.

"Come again," he said.

"The bishop. Do you think he'll get away with all of this?"

"I don't see why not. He's been getting away with it for twenty years, and by the looks of this place, he's made it work."

"That's not the way I figure it. I don't think it'll last."

"I don't follow."

"The way I see it, the bishop made a big mistake bringing in all us pros. Sure, the job'll get done better, but he's bound to attract attention. It's only a matter of time. Hell, I wouldn't be surprised if the Pinkertons were in town already."

"I wouldn't know much about that," Raider said.

"Just wait, you will."

Raider couldn't resist pressing the issue. "You've had trouble with Pinkerton?"

"A shitpot full but nothing I can't handle. I can smell a Pinkerton at fifty paces, and I always keep them one step behind."

"I seem to remember hearing that you met a couple of them real close once."

"You're talking about those Pinkertons in Missouri. They only got what was coming to them. They killed my stepbrother, who was nothing but a simple kid, and they blew my mama's arm right off her body. Put yourself in my place, Matt. What would you do to a man who maimed your own mother just because you were her son?"

"I'd kill him."

James nodded glumly.

"If you think Pinkerton might be in town, why are you staying?"

"I'm not. We're leaving right after the job tomorrow. If the Pinkertons are here, everybody'll leave. I wouldn't be surprised if the bishop ends up in the slammer before the week is out."

Raider grunted and said, "I figure I'll pull out of here myself soon. I'd just as soon avoid Pinkerton, too."

"Have you thought about my offer?"

"What offer?"

"Joining the James-Younger gang."

"I really haven't, Jesse. Let me sleep on it, and we'll talk again tomorrow. All right?"

"Sounds fair enough."

Raider spent the rest of the morning lounging around his room. He ventured out at noon to find something to eat. As he was about to enter the huge barroom, somebody called, "Hey, Pike, over here."

He turned to see a middle-aged man dressed in a very expensive gray vicuña suit with all the trimmings. "Come over here a minute," the man insisted. Raider went to the table, and the man extended his hand. "I'm Bill Raynor," he said.

Raider recognized the name. Bill Raynor was considered the baddest man in El Paso, a town with more than its share of lowlifes. He was also regarded as one of the fastest, straightest shooters alive, and the fact that a man with his life-style had lived past his fortieth year testified to the validity of his reputation.

"Pike, Matt Pike," Raider said.

"I know who you are," said Raynor. "I've made it my business to know every other fast gun before he knows me."

"That's right smart of you."

"Yeah. We don't work too far apart, you know. A lot of my friends have seen you in action around Little Rock. I've heard nothing but good things about you."

"Thank you," Raider said, ignoring the fact that Raynor was obviously lying.

"Why don't you come outside with me. We're about to play a little game."

"What sort of game?"

"Just follow me. You'll enjoy it, probably do right good at it."

They went outside and around the house to a thirty-acre field adjacent to the bishop's flower garden. Standing around talking were several of the outlaw guests: John Wesley Hardin, Dave Mather, Ike Clanton, Cole Younger, and a dozen others. Raynor walked to the front of the group.

"Okay boys," he said, "we haven't done much the last two weeks, and I don't have to tell you we have a big day ahead of us tomorrow. What do you say we practice and have ourselves some fun at the same time."

"How much?" asked Bill Longley, another Texas gunfighter.

"Let's make it sweeter this time," Raynor said. "Ten bucks a man."

"Which game are we playing, Bill?"

"What do you say to four corners?"

Raider had seen the game played once or twice but had never participated. It was played with bottles. One man stood in an open area, and four others formed a square around him. Each cornerman tossed a bottle high in the air while the man in the middle tried to shoot as many bottles as he could.

Raynor walked around holding two Stetsons. In one, each man deposited his $10 stake. From the other, each drew a number, indicating the order in which they would shoot. Raider drew number four.

Again Raynor spoke. "All right, this is winner take all. The boys who drew the high numbers will be the throwers first. I'll count off. Make sure you throw them high."

They took their places, and the competition began. Of the first three, only one man, Ike Clanton, hit more than one bottle. He hit two and walked off grinning.

Raider stepped in and slid his Remington in and out of its holster a few times to get the feel of it. Each of the throwers stood forty feet from him.

"Are you ready?" Raynor asked.

Raider nodded.

"One," Raynor yelled.

The bottle over Raider's right shoulder flew into the air. Raider shattered it as Raynor yelled, "Two." Raider whirled to his right and scored a direct hit on the second bottle. "Three" and "four" produced nothing but broken glass. He'd hit them all.

"Very good, Mr. Pike," Raynor said as Raider walked out of the ring with the same determined look he'd carried into it. He watched as the next seven men fared no better than Clanton. Then it was time for Dave Mather and John Wesley Hardin to enter the circle. Mather coolly hit all four, and Hardin did the same.

"Very impressive," shouted Raynor. "It looks like we'll have a three-way shootout to see who gets the cash."

They drew new numbers, and Raider's was high.

Raynor looked at the throwers and said, "No more than ten feet apart this time. Let's make it interesting."

Hardin stepped in first. Raynor rattled off the numbers much faster than previously, and the bottles weren't thrown as high. Hardin shot as fast as he could but managed to hit only the first one.

"It wasn't my day," he said as he calmly returned his gun to his holster and walked back to the house, not bothering to see how the competition turned out.

Mather was next. He stretched his arms several times to loosen his body and then said, "Okay."

Raynor shouted out the count. Mather hit the first bottle, missed the second, and then recovered to hit the third and fourth.

"Mighty good," said Raynor. "That round'll be tough to beat."

Raider stepped up, breathed deeply, and nodded. The count began, and the bottles flew. He hit the first three and then spun and fired at the fourth. He missed. But just as the crowd groaned, he fired again and shattered the bottle when it was only inches from the ground.

Mather's eyes nearly popped out of his head. "That's unfair," he shouted. "You're only allowed four shots."

Raynor said, "Nobody ever said that, Dave. It's just that I don't recall ever seeing anybody fast enough to take five shots before."

"I say we shoot again," Mather growled.

"I hit four," Raider said. "That's all there is to it."

"He's right, Dave," Raynor said. "He beat you fair and square."

Mather looked Raider in the eye. "You'll be sorry for this," he said.

He stormed into the house and slammed the door behind him. Several of the outlaws laughed, but Raider never cracked a smile.

"Don't worry about him," Raynor said as he handed Raider the money. "He's just a little sore, that's all. If I were you, I'd steer clear of him for a couple of days."

"Thanks," Raider said as he took the bills and stuffed them deep into his pocket.

After dinner, most of the outlaws headed for the Salt Lake Saloon. Raider had hoped to leave the bishop's quietly and stop at Emily's before going to the tavern. He waited until the others were gone, strapped on his belt and shoulder holsters, and stepped outside. As he was saddling his horse, Jesse James came into the barn.

"Matt, how are you doing?" he asked.

"All right."

"I understand you showed everybody up playing four corners today."

"You might say that."

"You heading for the saloon?"

"Yeah, I guess so."

"Good. I'll ride in with you."

As they headed for town, the sun was setting over the mountains.

"Mighty pretty country," said James.

"Uh huh."

"Still, I always feel a little uncomfortable when I leave Missouri."

"How do you mean?"

"You know, it's the life of the outlaw. There's never a moment's peace on the road. You never know who might be following you. You don't even know if the gent you're talking to or riding with will shoot you in the back if he gets a chance."

"And you figure it's different in Missouri?"

"No, not really. It's just that there's something special about being home. It makes me feel a little safer knowing that if a Pinkerton nailed me in my home state, I'd go out like a hero.''

"That means a lot to you, don't it?''

"Yeah, I suppose it does. There ain't much else to recommend being an outlaw.''

"Come on, Jesse, you told me yourself how much money you made last year and how much you're going to make on your next job. You're rich.''

"Sometimes I am, but a rich man doesn't sleep with his horse, and a rich man doesn't have to steal food from farmers' fields because somebody's chasing him and he doesn't dare go into town.''

"But you're a hero. That's what you want, ain't it?''

"I'm no hero. I've seen the dime novels and heard the songs, but what good is that? Twenty years from now, who's going to remember Jesse James?''

Raider shrugged.

"Nobody, that's who. I'm a married man, Matt. Zee is about the prettiest girl you ever did see, but I can't give her a life befitting a proper lady. I'd give anything to take some money, settle down, and raise horses, just me, Zee, and little Jesse, but I know I never will. My time will come up early. It's the price to be paid, and you'll pay it too, some day.''

"I reckon I will,'' Raider said, "but I promise you folks'll remember the name Jesse James long after they forget Matt Pike.''

James laughed. "Maybe they will, Matt, maybe they will.''

They rode in silence the rest of the way, and Raider considered the irony of the situation. Here he was riding with the man Pinkerton had established as its top priority. He knew he'd have no trouble apprehending the outlaw if he wanted to, but that would jeopardize the mission. He also knew that failure to capture Jesse would eliminate a golden opportunity to claim a $20,000 reward people had put up.

He glanced over at Jesse and rationalized that if Doc or even Allan Pinkerton himself were calling the shots, they'd let James go. It would be wrong to abandon a mission which could conceivably save hundreds of lives in order to collar a single outlaw, no matter what his status.

They rode past Emily's house, and Raider cast a quick glance toward it in the hope that he might see Doc. He saw no one, and they continued down the road.

As they entered the saloon, every head turned. Raider assumed that they were looking at James; even among other outlaws he was something of a legend. But Jesse said, "Looks like word's gotten around."

"About what?"

"These boys are mighty competitive when it comes to shooting. A fellow hits eight straight in four corners, he's going to have plenty of people talking about him."

They pushed through the crowd, and Raider realized that people were looking at him. He noticed a large table in the corner. Seated at it were people who'd been with Kid Cummings when Raider killed him, including several Dead Rabbits led by Yankee Sullivan, Mr. Schwartze, and Dave Mather. Raider didn't like the idea of Mather being with Sullivan.

Raider and James sat with Frank James and Cole Younger.

"Mr. Pike," said the elder James, "you've been a popular topic of conversation here this evening. I understand you put on a hell of a show this afternoon."

Raider smiled.

"Well," said Younger, "some folks wasn't so impressed." He motioned toward the table in the corner.

Raider had just finished a bourbon when Doc came through the door.

"Excuse me a minute," Raider said. He walked across

the floor and intercepted Doc as he was heading for the bar.

"What's up?" Doc asked.

"More than I can tell you here."

"Let's go back over to Emily's."

"I can't leave. I don't want to make anybody curious."

"You been getting into trouble again?"

"Not now, all right?"

"All right." Doc looked around and then said, "The bishop is in this thing up to his neck. I think Clint Stover was on to him, and Lee had him killed."

"I wouldn't be surprised. I talked with the bishop this morning."

"And?"

"I can't talk now. I wrote everything down in this here note." He handed Doc paper on which he'd scribbled before leaving for town.

"What about James?"

"I'm drinking with him right now. We rode into town together. He's a hell of a nice guy."

"He's a con man, Raider."

"I don't know, Doc."

"Raider, take it from another con man. Don't let him fool you."

"I reckon you're right. Anyway, just take this note and get out of here before somebody gets suspicious."

In the far corner of the room, Mysterious Dave Mather had gone into the sort of semidaze that had earned him his nickname, and his eyes were glued on Doc as he left the saloon.

"Has the devil gotten into you, boy?" Yankee Sullivan asked Mather, noticing his dreamy state.

"He was *born* with the Devil in him," said one of the Rabbits.

They all laughed.

Mather seemed oblivious to their comments and laughter and kept his eyes fixed on the door a full minute after Doc had passed through it. Finally, he said softly, "Well, I'll be."

"You'll be *what*, for Christ's sakes?" Sullivan asked before guzzling a glass of beer and wiping his mouth with his shirt-sleeve.

"I think we finally have that son of a bitch Pike where we want him."

"I want him six feet under," said Sullivan.

"That can be arranged," Mather said.

"Are you going to let us in on this?"

"Did you see that blond dude Pike was talking to?" Mather asked.

"He's a doctor," said Schwartze. "I think he's going around with the lady who lives in the house next to mine."

"He's no doctor," said Mather. "He's a Pinkerton."

"What the hell are you talking about?" snapped Sullivan.

"It was a lot of years ago and a long way from here, but I remember."

"You're sure?" the Dead Rabbits' leader asked.

"Yup, sure as shit. Must have been ten years ago in Dodge City. He captured the fellow who taught me everything I know. I'll never forget his face."

"What do we do?" asked Schwartze. "Should we blow the whistle on him?"

"That's too good for the likes of Pike," said Sullivan. "I'll kill him myself."

"What about the Pinkerton?"

"We'll leave that up to Mr. Schwartze."

"What do you mean?" Schwartze asked.

"The lady. Take care of the lady, and I promise you her Pinkerton friend will come running." Mather raised his glass and added, "To Matt Pike, gentlemen. This will be the last toast he'll ever receive, at least as a live man."

CHAPTER TWENTY

Raider was awakened by a commotion in the hall. It was pitch black; he couldn't see his hand in front of his face. As the noise grew louder, he remembered that it was time for the raid on the wagon train. Somebody banged on his door and shouted, "Get up! Time to go to work."

Raider dragged himself out of bed and threw on the same clothes he'd worn the night before. He stepped into the hall and saw people coming out of their rooms and heading for the barroom. He went back inside, strapped on his holsters, and followed the crowd.

There was a buzz of excitement in the room when Raider arrived. Bishop Lee was standing on the bar. He looked out over the crowd until the room was completely quiet.

"All right, gentlemen," he said, "all I ask is one little favor every couple of weeks, and this week it's a bunch of Germans heading out to California. My scout says it's a big wagon train and should be loaded. Remember, the first rule is no survivors. If we keep leaving survivors, some-body's going to catch on to us . . . to *me*." Lee smiled, cleared his throat, and continued. "Okay, gentlemen, let's get into our disguises."

Raider followed the others to several crates near the bar from which they picked out suitable clothing for the raid. Raider chose a pair of buckskin pants and an ivory necklace. Bare chested, he walked to a middle-aged woman who was applying war paint and helping men fit into wigs.

"What do you think *you're* doing?" she asked Raider.

Raider frowned.

"Did you ever see an Indian with fair skin and a hairy chest?"

"Nope."

"Then go put on a shirt. And while you're at it, take off that holster and those boots. You can go barefoot."

Raider did what he was told.

"Much better," she said. She painted his face and fitted him with a long, black wig. "Atta boy, pretty as a picture. Next!"

Raider watched as the others were transformed into Indians. When Jesse James was through, he came to Raider.

"How do you like this?" he asked, laughing and pointing to a headdress he was wearing. "They went and made me a chief."

"Not bad," Raider said, "not bad."

An hour later, everyone was ready to go. The bishop hopped up on the bar again and said, "We'll divide into three groups led by me, Dave Mather, and John Wesley Hardin. Each of those men has a list of who's in their group and what the duties are."

Mather scanned his list and then conferred with Hardin. Each took out a pencil and made adjustments in their rosters. Mather looked out toward Raider, grinned wickedly, glanced down at his list again and read it aloud. Matt Pike was the last name he called. Most of the Dead Rabbits were also in his contigent.

The group moved outside, where servants had brought

horses to the front of the house. The men mounted up and headed for their appointment with the German wagon train.

Raider thought of Doc and the note he'd given him. He knew that Doc hadn't had enough time to assemble the necessary manpower to stop the attacks, but he might have thought to head off the wagon train and persuade the Germans to change direction and avert a slaughter.

The predawn glow grew brighter as the group moved circuitously around the town. In the distance, Raider could make out the outline of Daniel Edmonds's palatial estate, and he briefly thought of the attack this same group had made on his own wagon train in which Agnes was killed. He clenched his teeth and forced the thought from his mind.

They reached a narrow pass, and the group fell into a single file. The pass ended in a clearing.

"This is it," said the bishop. "Let's get to work."

They split into groups and headed in three separate directions. Mather's group was designated to remain on the nearby ridge as marksmen.

Few of the men said anything as they stayed in position for nearly two hours, anticipating the wagon train. With each passing minute Raider became more convinced that Doc had succeeded in intercepting the Germans. Then, just before eight o'clock, he heard a rumbling in the distance. Everyone looked up.

"This is it," said the bishop.

Those designated to ride mounted their horses and moved into an orderly formation. The others stayed on their bellies, guns loaded and in their hands. Raider glanced around nervously. He had no idea what to do. Obviously, Doc had not reached the wagon train, and Raider knew that he could not take part in the massacre of innocent people. On the other hand, he was aware that if he didn't, he'd be shot on the spot by the outlaws.

He hated to admit it, but it was time to run, to retreat, to hightail it out of there as fast as humanly possible. But something inside him made him pause. As the last wagon reached the clearing, he jerked his rifle to his shoulder and squeezed off a round. His aim was true. It knocked the hat off the driver of the last wagon, sending him diving for cover and startling others in the train out of their morning reverie.

Hoping that his warning would save a few lives, Raider now attended to his own. He leaped to his feet, vaulted onto his horse, kicked his bare heels into the gelding's girth, and bolted to a start. Behind him he heard the bishop roar, "Go," and the gang swarmed over the hill. Mather, realizing Raider's betrayal, spun around and fired at the retreating rider. The shot whizzed past Raider's cheek, took off the tip of his earlobe, and crashed into the barrel of his rifle, knocking it from his hands. There was no time to turn and retrieve it as he urged the animal to top speed.

Mather was left with only Clanton to protect the ridge as a group of Germans headed for it. Mather knew that if he went after Raider, the whole assault would be in jeopardy.

"Fucking bastard," he shouted as he turned his attention to the onrushing Germans and opened fire.

Raider stopped briefly, looked back, and surveyed the carnage. A young blond woman attempting to run to safety sprawled to the ground when a bullet found her chest. A red stain quickly spread over the white bodice of her dress. Seconds later, an eight-year-old girl who was following her was hit in the mouth with a shotgun shell. Her face was torn away, and pieces of it flew through the air. Raider had seen enough. Infuriated that he'd had to leave his pistols behind when he'd changed into the Indian dress, he rode full steam in the direction of Daniel Edmonds's spread. Behind him, two figures raised a cloud of dust as they tried to narrow the gap between themselves and Raider's disappearing image on the horizon.

Raider reached Edmonds's house, turned, and caught sight of the dust cloud made by his pursuers. He flew from the saddle, leaving the horse untethered, and pounded on the door for what seemed like an eternity. Finally, the maid opened it and Raider charged into the house, slamming the door behind him.

"Who are you?" the maid shouted. "What is the meaning of this?"

"It's me, Raider," he said, pulling the black Indian wig from his head. "Where's Molly's room?"

"Mr. Raider, Molly is now a married woman. You can't just barge in here, even in disguise. You'll compromise her."

Raider grabbed her by the shoulders and shook her. "Where is her room, damn it?"

"Top of the stairs, first door on the right."

He charged up the stairs and into the room, ran to the bed, and shook Molly. She slowly opened her eyes.

"Raider," she said, rubbing them. "Why are you dressed like that?"

"Get up quick, honey," he said. "I need you real bad."

"You're wounded," she said, reaching up to touch his bloody ear. "Let me get something to fix it."

"No time, Molly. Do you have a gun?"

Responding to the urgency in his voice, she got up, ran to her bureau, and drew a pistol from the top drawer. She pressed it into Raider's hand.

"It's loaded," she said.

"Come on," he said, dragging her from the room. "Chances are, a bunch of bad hombres are breathing down my neck, and I'm going to need all the help I can get."

As they ran downstairs, Raider spotted a shotgun hanging over the fireplace. He grabbed it and reached the window just in time to see two Dead Rabbits, O'Brien and Donnelly, approaching the house.

"Good," Raider whispered. "There's only two of them. I'll take the one on the left, you nail the one on the right." He handed her back the pistol. "If we do it right, they'll never even get off a round. Just wait till I give the word."

Daniel Edmonds came out of his room and stood on the landing. "What's going on here?" he shouted, Receiving no answer, he started down the stairs.

"Now," yelled Raider.

He pulled the trigger on the shotgun, and blood erupted from five holes in O'Brien's face, soaking the front of his shirt. Molly fired, too, but her gun kicked up and the bullet sailed over Donnelly's head, barely grazing his scalp. Donnelly managed to get off a shot just as Raider's second round peppered his chest and pierced his heart. The outlaw's bullet tore past Molly's shoulder.

"That was a close one," she said, smiling into Raider's eyes.

They turned and walked toward the staircase where Edmonds was sitting halfway down the stairs, his head thrown back and his eyes closed.

"Would you look at that," Molly said, shaking her head. "He's the only fellow I know who can fall asleep right in the middle of a gunfight."

"I'm not so sure he's sleeping, Molly," Raider said as he observed Edmonds's fluttering eyelids. "Look at this." He pulled back the folds of Edmonds's silk dressing gown to reveal a gaping wound in his gut made by Donnelly's last round.

Edmonds moaned, opened his eyes, and managed a weak smile up at Raider.

"What'll we do?" Molly asked.

Other brides came running to see what had happened. Ann was the last to arrive.

"Did Raider shoot him?" she asked Molly.

"No, I haven't shot him," Raider said disgustedly.

"Raider?" Molly's eyes were pleading.

"Let's get him to the sofa," Raider said, helpless to come up with another suggestion.

"Shouldn't we bring him to a doctor?" Ann asked.

Raider looked down at Edmonds. "How do you feel?"

"My stomach hurts real bad."

"I can't take you to a doctor. The ride would be too dangerous. We'll try to find Doc Hastings, but I'm afraid he's about to be mighty busy. Another wagon train was hit this morning."

There was loud knocking at the front door. Raider backed up against a wall next to it, the shotgun ready.

"Answer it," he said.

Molly went to the door and opened it. "Yes?"

"I'm looking for Mr. Raider . . ."

"Doc," said Raider, putting the gun down. "What in hell are you doing here?"

"You're a doctor?" Molly exclaimed.

"Not exactly."

"Edmonds has been shot, Doc. I don't want to move him."

"Where is he?"

"On the sofa."

Doc examined the wound. "It's just one bullet," he said, "but it's in a bad spot."

"I know," Raider said.

"Best thing to do is to yank it."

"You mean you'll pull it out?" Molly asked. "I thought you said you weren't a doctor."

"I'm not, but I've done this before, and it's the only chance he's got. Get me a tweezer and some alcohol."

Molly rushed off and returned with the supplies Doc had requested. He poured alcohol onto the tweezers, turned to Raider, and said, "Give me a bullet."

The big man emptied one from Molly's pistol and handed it to his partner.

"Mr. Edmonds," said Doc loudly, "I'd like you to bite on this because it'll hurt like hell when I pull the shell. This will help take your mind off it."

Edmonds was only semiconscious. "Is it round?" he muttered.

"Sort of."

"No, thank you, I can't stand round things in my mouth."

Doc looked over at Raider with a puzzled expression. Raider shrugged and raised his eyebrows. Doc went to work and found the bullet with relative ease. He managed to get the tweezers on it. He tugged, and the bullet came free. Blood now poured out of Edmonds in a red river.

"Pass me the bandages," Doc said. Raider bent down and handed him the pieces of torn sheets Molly had fetched to dress the wound. Doc finished the job and stood. "I wrapped it as tight as I could," he said. "We'll just have to hope for the best. If he stops bleeding, we'll get him into town or get Doc Hastings to come out here to see him."

The girls huddled around Edmonds as Raider and Doc went to a corner of the room.

"How did you know I was here?" Raider asked.

"I didn't, just a hunch. I rode over and saw your horse wandering around out front. I also saw two dead bodies and figured you might have had something to do with that."

"Why didn't you stop the wagon train?"

"I didn't get a chance. Besides, something's happened to Emily."

"What?"

"I'm not sure. I stayed at the hotel last night. I came to her house before sunup, and she was gone. The door was wide open, and some furniture was knocked over. I don't know what anybody would want with her, but I know she didn't leave on her own."

"Wait a minute," Raider said.

"What is it?"

"Schwartze."

"What about him?"

"All the gunslingers were in on the raid this morning except Schwartze, but he was with us last night and saw me talking to you."

"You think Schwartze has Emily?"

"It ain't a bad bet."

CHAPTER TWENTY-ONE

Doc and Raider looked back in the direction of the ambush after they'd mounted up in front of Edmonds's house. A large cloud of dust bellowed from the clearing and settled in the still Utah air. They stared for a moment and then slapped their horses on the rumps and raced to Schwartze's house.

Doc banged on it. There was no answer. He tried turning the knob, but the door was locked. He took a step back, lowered his shoulder, and hit the door with the full weight of his body. It sagged but remained secure. He dusted himself off and prepared to repeat the action.

"Wait a minute," said Raider. "Let me try."

"Just hurry," Doc said, taking out a pistol and checking to make sure that its chambers were full.

Raider still wore his Indian garb from that morning. He'd washed his face and left his wig at Edmonds, but he was still wearing the buckskins and was barefoot. He looked down at his feet and said, "I could use those big old boots about now."

"For Christ sake, Raider, Emily could be dead in there. Just knock down the fucking door."

The big Pinkerton charged like a runaway farm horse, and the door gave way. He tumbled into the room, did a somersault, and landed on his feet, guns drawn. He saw nothing.

Doc slowly followed Raider into the house. The sun was now high in the sky, but all the curtains were closed tight; it seemed more like dusk inside.

They approached the door to the kitchen with caution. Doc stood to the side as Raider kicked it open and burst in. What they saw caused their stomachs to turn inside out. A female body hung from the ceiling on a meat hook. Its legs had been hacked off from just above the knees. A bluish color permeated whatever skin wasn't encrusted in dried blood. The breasts and surrounding area had been crudely butchered, almost as though the flesh had been torn out with bare hands. The face was unmistakable to Raider.

"Jesus fucking Jesus," he growled, "it's Agnes."

"Who?" Doc asked. He gagged at the stench.

"Agnes. The old lady I came out here with."

"Why would Schwartze kill her?"

"He didn't. Remember, I left the body at the side of the road, and when I went back for it, it was gone?"

"Right."

"It looks like Schwartze was the one who took her."

"But why?" Doc mumbled. Then he said, "Hold on a minute."

"What's the matter?" Raider asked.

"Packer," Doc said. "Alfred Packer. Don't you remember?"

"The one Wagner told us about a couple of years ago when we were out in Colorado? He showed us his picture, didn't he?"

"Right. Packer was the one who took a couple of boys out on a prospecting job and killed them."

"So?"

"He ate them, Raider. Packer is a goddamn cannibal."

"Cannibal? You think that this guy Packer is Schwartze and that he eats people?"

A muffled scream came from the next room. Doc rushed toward it, but just before he reached it a gleaming meat cleaver hurtled through the darkness at him. He ducked, and the cleaver sliced through a wall.

Before Doc could regain his stance, Schwartze was on top of him, wielding an even bigger ax. As he raised it above his head with both hands, Raider bolted across the room and upset him just enough to keep him from driving the cleaver into Doc's skull. The razor-sharp ax did strike Doc's shoulder, though, and he grabbed at it in pain.

Schwartze, who still held the weapon, tried shifting his weight under Raider so that he could use the cleaver on him, but Raider grabbed him by the wrist and brutally slammed it to the floor. Schwartze let go, and the cleaver fell from his hand. He looked up at the Pinkerton, his eyes glazed and crazed.

Raider sat on his chest and glanced over at Doc, whose hand and arm were soaked in blood. Raider could see through the doorway to the kitchen where the ghoulish figure of Agnes Griffin swung from the ceiling. He shook with rage, picked up the cleaver with one hand, and gripped Schwartze's throat with the other.

Doc watched silently. His every instinct was to stop Raider's impulsive action, but something inside wouldn't allow him to speak. It seemed an eternity as Raider and Schwartze stared into each other's eyes: Raider's filled with hate, Schwartze's round and flickering with dementia. Raider brought the edge of the blade a few inches from Schwartze's neck. Schwartze began to laugh, the uncontrollable cackle of a lunatic filling the room. Raider touched the blade to the madman's Adam's apple and drew blood. Then he tossed the cleaver to the floor, spat in Schwartze's face, and stood. Schwartze stopped laughing and started to cry.

"You okay?" Raider asked.

"I'll live," Doc said. "It's not as bad as it looks."

Raider tied Schwartze while Doc went into the bedroom, where Emily was bound and gagged in a chair. He pulled off the gag and said, "Did that bastard hurt you, honey?"

"Oh, Doc, I'm so glad to see you. You'd never believe some of the things he did to . . . to that *thing* in the kitchen. He cooked parts of her body and ate it. He . . . he tried to make me eat it, too."

"Don't worry, honey, it's all over."

"Last night, Doc, he took the body off the hook and brought it into bed with him. He acted as though she were alive. It was the most horrifying, disgusting thing I ever saw." She fell into his arms and sobbed.

"It's all right, Emily, there's nothing to worry about anymore. The whole thing is over, I promise you."

"Just get me out of here, Doc. Please, just take me home."

"Okay."

"And promise you won't leave me, Doc. I couldn't stand seeing you leave now."

"I'm not going anywhere yet, baby." He took her by the arm and escorted her out of the house, turning to Raider and saying, "You take care of Schwartze, then meet me at Emily's."

"Will do."

She cleansed and bandaged his shoulder wound when they got to her house. Then she started crying again.

"What is it?" Doc asked.

"I don't know, I guess everything. First you showed up and I started to live again. Next thing I know, I'm worrying about you the way I used to worry about Clint. Then a bunch of dead Frenchmen are in my house. I could take all that, but . . .''

''But what?''

''Then you tell me Clint might have been murdered. I hardly have a chance to get over that when I'm kidnaped in the middle of the night by a . . . a . . .''

''I know, Emily,'' Doc said, sitting next to her and putting his arms around her.

''I just don't know what to make of it all.''

''Neither do I, but try not to cry. That isn't going to help anything.''

''I'm not so sure about that.''

The door opened, and Raider came through it. ''How's everything?'' he asked.

Doc ignored the question and asked instead, ''Where's Schwartze?''

''You mean Packer,'' said Raider. ''The sheriff's got him locked up. He showed me the file on him. He came to Salt Lake after escaping from Los Piños. They say he murdered and ate five guys along the Gunnison over in Colorado and stole a couple of thousand bucks from them, too. The law's been looking for Packer for a long time.''

''And he's been right under their nose all along, just changed his name.''

''That's about the size of it.''

Doc walked into the kitchen and made tea for Emily. He handed her her cup and said to Raider, ''I never got a chance to hear about this morning. What happened with the Indian raid?''

''Right, I almost forgot. It was the bloodiest mess I ever saw. They shot everybody down like animals.''

''How'd you manage to get out of it?''

''I hate to admit it, Doc, but I ran my ass out of there, went straight to Edmonds's place. Two Dead Rabbits came after me. That's how Edmonds got shot.''

"I wonder how he's doing."

"No way to tell, but he looked pretty bad to me. The gut's a bad place to catch one." Raider walked over to the window, pulled back the curtain, and looked outside. "What the hell's going on out there?" he muttered.

"Where?" asked Doc.

"A whole bunch of people are riding up to the hotel. Looks like some sort of convention."

Doc rushed to the window. "It is," he said, grinning, "a Pinkerton convention."

"What do you mean?"

"I telegraphed Wagner and told him to send help. I figured it was just a matter of time until guys as smart as Jesse James realize they're drawing too much attention and hightail it. We have to act now if we're going to stop them." He looked out the window again and shook his head. "I'll be." He chuckled. "I have to hand it to Wagner. It looks like he sent every Pinkerton west of the Mississippi."

"Then why are we standing around?"

They went in to the living room, checked their guns, and put on their jackets. Doc kissed Emily good-bye and told her that he'd be back soon. They got to the hotel, pushed through a crowd of operatives on the steps, and made their way to the desk.

"Well, where is he?" they heard a man ask a clerk.

"I'm sure Dr. Weatherbee would not want me telling every angry mob that comes in here where he can be found," the clerk answered nervously.

"There's a lot of truth in that," Doc said.

The man who'd asked for Doc spun around at the sound of his voice. "Doc, how are you?" he asked. He was a tall, blond man with a handlebar moustache.

"Not bad, Noah, but we got real trouble." Doc took

him aside. "They got more outlaws up here than you ever saw in one place before."

"Like?"

"Jesse and Frank James, Cole Younger, Mather, Hardin, Ringo, McClowerys, Clantons, Raynor, Longley, Lowe, just about anybody else worth mentioning."

"How do you want to handle it?"

Doc shrugged and said, "Just as long as we do it fast. Hang on a second." He turned to Raider. "What do you think, partner?"

Raider frowned and said, "They just come back from one of their raids. If I know them, that'll mean a big party. If we can get up there and take them by surprise, we just might be able to nail all of them."

"It's your show, Doc," Noah said.

Doc looked at Raider and smiled. "It's *your* show, partner," he said. "Lead the way."

They stepped out onto the porch, and Raider addressed them. "We're going up there," he said, "and if we pull this off, we'll cut crime in the West in half. I don't need to tell anybody how important this thing is or how dangerous these boys are. The only way we're going to take them is to work together and do things by the book. The last thing we need is a pack of glory hounds trying to be the one who captures Jesse James."

The crowd murmured its approval.

"Okay, let's go. When we get there, you'll be taking orders from me." He looked at Doc. "And from Doc, too. Good luck."

They rode in formation to the bishop's estate. It was deathly quiet when they arrived; none of the servants who usually mingled outside were visible.

"I don't like the looks of this," Raider said.

"What's wrong?" Doc asked.

"Too quiet."

"If it's a big party, Raider, they're probably all inside."

"Maybe," said Raider, "or maybe they saw us coming and are ready for us."

"Let's split up," said Noah.

Doc agreed. "I'll take a group around back. Noah, you stay out front. Raider, set up a few boys on either side so we have them hemmed in. The group in front will fire over the roof to attract attention. When they rush to the front, we open up from the sides and rear. Got it?"

Everyone nodded.

Five minutes later, Noah gave the order and his men fired a volley well above the bishop's roof. There was no response. One of the men in Raider's group stood.

"This is bullshit," he said. "I can go right through that side door."

"They'll blow you away," Raider said.

"I've done it a hundred times before."

"Not with boys like this you haven't. Besides, you heard me. We stick to the book. You're not going to get your glory here."

"Listen, Raider, Jesse James is in there, and nobody's going to stop me from taking my best shot."

Suddenly, without warning, he delivered a roundhouse right. Raider ducked and felt it whiz by his ear. He responded with his own right to the gut and a quick left to the mouth that dropped the other Pinkerton to the ground.

"Anybody else want to break the rules?" Raider asked.

He was answered with silence, and all eyes returned to Bishop Lee's mansion.

Noah said to his group of operatives, "Fire a little lower this time, into the roof." Weapons exploded, sending pieces of the roof into the air. Still there was no response.

A minute later the front door flew open, and the sound of clinking Pinkerton hammers filled the air. A sobbing maid, her hands high above her head, stepped through the door. "There is nobody here," she yelled. "They have all gone away."

None of the Pinkertons answered. They knew that it could be a trick.

The maid yelled again, "Please, don't shoot. It is only me and my friends. The men have all gone away."

"Gone where?" yelled Noah.

"I do not know. Please, don't kill me. I have nothing to do with these bad people."

The Pinkertons looked at each other. Someone had to check the house. Raider looked at the operative he'd flattened, who was still on the ground.

"Well?" Raider asked.

The downed Pinkerton stayed put.

Raider drew a deep breath and stepped over the ridge, his Winchester .44 in his left hand, his right hand on the Remington 30-30 on his hip. Slowly, he made his way to where the maid stood. Doc joined him.

"I think she's right," Doc said. "I don't see anybody else."

They went inside. The door to the barroom was open, and the halls were deserted. Aside from a few frightened servants, the place was unquestionably empty.

They returned outside and were about to wave off the assault, when Doc said, "Wait a minute." He pointed to a large barn adjacent to the mansion.

"You think they could be hiding in there?" Raider asked.

"Let's find out."

They approached the barn cautiously. Doc stood to one side of the door, Raider on the other. They'd been together too long to have to discuss plans in such situations. Doc licked his lips, nodded once, and kicked open the door. Raider dove through the opening, ready to shoot.

"It's empty," he growled, disappointed.

"Not even horses?"

"Empty."

Doc kicked the dirt. "It's like I said, Raider, they're too smart to let this happen. They're gone."

Raider picked up a rock and hurled it against a wall. "Damn it," he yelled.

CHAPTER TWENTY-TWO

"Raider, it's good to see you."

"Hello, Ann. You remember Doc Weatherbee, don't you?"

"I certainly do. Come in."

The two Pinkertons entered Daniel Edmonds's home.

"How is he?" Raider asked.

"It's so blooming hard to tell. He keeps having attacks of his narcolepsy or whatever it's called. We think he's dead, and then a minute later he snaps out of it."

"What did Dr. Hastings say?" Doc asked.

"He's in there with him now."

"Can we go in?" asked Raider.

"Sure, why not?"

She opened the door to Edmonds's bedroom, and Doc and Raider followed her inside. Molly and one of the other brides sat in chairs by an open window. Hastings was on the edge of the bed.

"Gentlemen," he said, standing.

"Good morning, Doctor," they said.

"Doctor," asked Raider, "can I talk to Mr. Edmonds a minute? I mean, can he hear me?"

"Oh, he can hear you all right," Hastings said, "and he can speak with you if he wishes."

Raider went to the bed and looked into Edmonds's face. It was pale, and his lips were dry.

"I just want to apologize, sir," Raider said.

Edmonds opened his eyes and said, "Apologize?" His voice was so weak that it was barely audible. "What for?"

"For the way I barged in here this morning. I feel responsible for what happened to you."

"No, Mr. Raider, we're responsible for ourselves in this world. You did what you had to, and I tried to do the same."

"That's very decent of you."

"Besides, I understand you're something of a hero. Tell me, is what they say about the bishop really true?"

"I'm afraid it is."

"I don't understand why he'd do such a thing. He was always kind to me."

"I reckon he's just plain greedy. Some folks are."

"I donated thousands of dollars to the church at his request. God only knows how many people died because of it."

"Don't blame yourself."

Edmonds began coughing, and Raider glanced at Hastings, who responded with a tight-lipped shake of the head.

Doc and Raider stepped out of the room, and Hastings followed them.

"How's it look, Doctor?" Doc asked.

"There's nothing I can do. He's bleeding internally. I'm trying to keep him comfortable for whatever time he might have left."

"Sorry to hear it," Doc said.

Raider and Doc left Edmonds's house and rode slowly

back into town. The sun was high, and the path on which they rode seemed drier and dustier than usual.

Raider, who was now dressed in his customary denims, shirt, leather jacket, and Stetson, said, "I should have left on those Indian clothes. They're a hell of a lot more comfortable than these."

They reached the town's main street, and Doc pulled back on the reins. "We've been working hard," he said. "What do you say we go up to my room, wash up, grab a bite, and relax?"

"I reckon it wouldn't do any harm."

As they entered the hotel, Raider asked. "How do you know the maid wasn't lying when she said Lee didn't leave with the outlaws?"

"Lee leaving Salt Lake City would be like taking away Dave Mather's gun. Without it, he's nothing. Lee's whole power base is the church. He gets everything from the Mormons, and I bet he's doing his damndest to round up support from his Mormon friends before we find him."

"Support or no support, he's mine," Raider said, and Doc knew that he meant it.

They walked up the stairs and headed for Doc's room. Standing in the doorway was the young priest Raider had seen at the bishop's place.

"Watch it, Doc," he said, "this is one of Lee's boys." His right hand went to his holster.

"Dr. Weatherbee?" the young man asked shyly.

"How do you know my name?"

"I'm here to explain that."

"Well, since you're one of Lee's boys, you'd better start explaining fast."

"You don't understand," the young priest said. "I'm not one of Bishop Lee's 'boys.' Not really. I'm the one who hired you."

Doc's face reflected his incredulity.

"Several members of the congregation put up the money, and I contacted Chicago. You see, Doctor, we knew several months ago that something unsavory was going on with the bishop. In the last few weeks it became painfully obvious to us, but we couldn't risk upsetting the bishop because . . . well, because we were afraid of what his reaction might be."

"So you let Pinkerton do it?"

"Yes."

"Well," Doc said, "that's all well and good except for one thing. I don't understand what you're doing here now. Why did you finally decide to come forward after we'd figured it out for ourselves?"

"Today's a holiday in our religion."

"So?"

"I just found out that Bishop Lee is going to hold holiday services in the church."

"That's crazy," Raider said.

"Not really, sir. He's convinced that people will rally around him. He plans to give them a sermon that will make him look like a saint and make you gentlemen look like devils."

"Will the people got for it?" Doc asked.

"I really can't say. The bishop is very persuasive when he wants to be."

"What time does this service start?"

The priest looked at a pocket watch. "In forty-five minutes."

"Okay, son, thanks for your help."

The priest left, and the Pinkertons went to Doc's room, where Doc changed into a fresh suit and Raider washed up. They went to the hotel dining room.

"Can you bring us a fast stack of hotcakes and a pot of coffee?" Doc asked a waitress. "Something troubling you?"

Doc asked his partner as they waited for their order. "I've never seen you look so nervous."

"I was just thinking."

"About what?"

"A lot of things, this whole dumb assignment, this whole stupid job. Last night I was riding down a dark road with Jesse James, the most famous outlaw in the West, the gunslinger everybody in the world is looking for."

"And?"

"I could've taken him, Doc, could've taken him easy. All I had to do was pull my gun and I would've been $20,000 richer, and Jesse James would have been out of everybody's hair for good."

"Why didn't you?"

"That's one of the things that bothers me. I don't know why. He trusted me. He was, you know, like a friend, and there are things a friend just don't do, things that just ain't right."

"*That's* why you didn't take him?"

"Hell, no. I knew you'd get all riled up if I took Jesse and ruined the assignment."

"You did right, Raider. You went by the book, and I'm proud of you."

"Doc, every outlaw worth anything, every gunslinger Pinkerton wants, has been right here under our nose, and we let them get away. I don't see that as something to be proud of."

Doc sighed. "Raider, we were hired to clear up the situation in Salt Lake City and with the Mormon church. We already bagged Packer. He's in jail. All we have to do now is get Lee. That's what we were hired for. This guy's killed hundreds of people, maybe more. He may not be as glamorous as Jesse James, but that's not important. Sure, you could have grabbed Jesse if you wanted to, maybe Hardin and Mather, too. You would have stolen some headlines and gotten a pat on the back from a lot of people, but we wouldn't have done our job. Lee would still be hitting wagon trains and killing people, and God only knows what Packer would be doing and who he'd be doing it to.''

The waitress arrived with their food and put it on the table.

"Maybe you're right," Raider said, "but I'll tell you one thing for sure."

"What's that?"

"I'm taking Lee. I don't care if I got to shoot every Mormon in Salt Lake City, I'll do it."

"Come on, Raider, you can't go shooting up a whole church and town."

"I'm taking him, Doc. If they let him go, fine, but if they don't they better be ready to fight for him."

Doc knew that it was futile to argue with him. They ate quickly, paid the bill and left the dining room.

"What do we do now?" Raider asked.

"Let's take the bull by the horns," Doc said. "We'll wait until the church is full, then go in and call him for what he is."

"Sounds good to me. Let's go."

They rode to the church, a simple wooden building with white paint that was fading fast from the constant sun and salty air. Parishioners filed into it. When it was filled, the sounds of a steam organ filled the countryside.

"Let's go," said Doc.

They dismounted and walked thirty feet to the church's steps. They looked at each other, nodded, and then walked through the open door. Many heads in the congregation turned to look at them. The faces were anything but friendly. Lee was at the altar and smiling at the organist. Apparently, he was unaware of their presence. When he did notice them, his face did not change expression. He smiled and nodded to the organist.

The music stopped, and Lee strode to the alter.

"Friends," he said in a resonant voice, "shall we begin?" He leafed through a booklet in his hands.

Doc's voice bellowed from the rear of the church. "I think we're about to end something instead of beginning it."

A murmur shot through the pews.

"Why, Dr. Weatherbee?" Lee asked, his voice brimming with strength and confidence.

Doc surveyed the angry faces looking in his direction. He announced, "We're Pinkerton operatives, and we have proof that you, Bishop Lee, are responsible for hundreds of immigrants being slaughtered, beginning with Mountain Meadows twenty years ago and ending this morning. We intend to see that you hang for it."

Raider and Doc headed up the center aisle. A half dozen Mormon men sprang from their seats and blocked their path. Raider stretched his fingers and caressed his gun.

"Give the bishop a chance to talk," one of the men said.

"Bishop?" Doc said.

"Surely you jest," the bishop bellowed. "I am the pillar of the greatest church in the world. Who are you, Dr. Weatherbee? A stranger to our midst, a stranger trying to upset a harmonious situation for your own personal glory. It is no secret that killers and thieves stayed in my own home. It is the way of God. I am a forgiving person, sir. Surely, it is no crime to show a lost soul the way of God. If it is, then I must plead guilty to that crime, but it is a crime of your world, not in a church of God."

"Murder is a crime anywhere you find it, Bishop."

"You accuse me of murder? Every man and woman in this congregation knows and approves of my rehabilitation program. They knew from the start that there might be crimes committed by the penitents. They accept it and sacrifice for it.''

"Cut it out, Lee," Raider screamed. "I was there. I saw you and your henchmen gun down innocent people. I've seen your wild parties for your friends. I've seen it all, and you're not going to get away with it.''

He took a menacing step forward but was restrained by three of the men. He knocked one down, and pandemonium erupted in the church. As Raider was about to coldcock another Mormon, the young priest to whom they'd spoken earlier leaped to the altar.

"Please, stop," he shouted. "Please, listen to what I have to say."

The scuffling stopped as the priest said, "What I have to say will be very difficult. I have not said it before for the same reason that each of you is protecting Bishop Lee: out of loyalty to the Church of the Latter Day Saints."

The church fell deathly still.

"The time to stop this misplaced loyalty is right now. We have confused loyalty to God with loyalty to Bishop Lee. I myself have hired these Pinkerton agents because we have an obligation to the *truth*. Truth is our *greatest* obligation, and as sad as it makes me to admit it, these men are telling the truth. Bishop Lee is a cold-blooded murderer. I have witnessed his ruthless actions."

"He's a liar," Lee shouted. "He wants only to rise to my position. He's a blasphemer."

A member of the congregation stood. "I put up some of the money for Pinkerton," he said. "I did it because I knew in my heart that Bishop Lee was dishonest."

"I was against this outlaw thing from the beginning," testified another Mormon. "I never saw one of them ever come to church."

"We'll recover," said the young priest. "We don't need Bishop Lee. We only need faith in *God*!"

Lee grabbed the priest and threw him to the floor. He looked out over the shocked congregation and buried his head in his hands. Raider walked between the men who had impeded him and went to the altar. He took out a pair of handcuffs and slapped them on the bishop's wrists.

"That's it Lee," he said. "It's all over."

The congregation understood. It did nothing to interfere.

CHAPTER TWENTY-THREE

Molly sat in a huge upholstered chair in the center of Daniel Edmonds's living room. Her feet were tucked under her like a little girl's.

"I don't really believe all the things that have happened to me," she said. "A short while ago I'd never left my village, and now, all of a sudden, I've crossed a continent. In my whole life I'd never seen people die, and the next thing I know, I'm shooting at people and killing them."

"You were just protecting yourself, honey," Raider said.

"He's right," said one of the other brides.

"I know, but seeing Agnes and then Daniel die has been terrible."

"He might have been a queer duck," said Ann, "but he was basically a nice man. He treated us like queens."

"That's right," said Molly. "He never did anything to hurt us." The brides looked at each other. "You know what the best thing about coming to America was?" Molly continued. "You people. Everybody's been so nice to me that I've almost forgotten how hard times have been." She looked at Raider. "Especially you," she said. "I don't know what I would have done without you. You've been like a father to me.'' She smiled. ''I mean like a big brother.'' She came to Raider and hugged him. ''You know, Raider, you're a very decent bloke.''

Raider blushed as he said, ''Don't let it get around, understand?'' The girls all laughed. ''I'm a little worried about you girls,'' he added.

''About what?'' Ann asked.

''Well, Edmonds is dead. You're in a new country with no husband.''

The brides looked at each other and giggled.

''What's so funny?'' Raider asked.

''Should we tell him?''

''Tell me what?'' Raider demanded.

''You mean you haven't heard, Raider? It's all over town.''

''Damn it, Ann, tell me.''

''Edmonds had left all of his money to the church, but when he heard what was going on, he changed his will.''

''So?''

''So, he left his wives $45 million.''

''Forty-five million?''

''You got it.'' laughed Ann. ''Why don't you stick around? It might be a lot of fun. You'll never have to work again. We'll take good care of you, just as you took good care of us.''

''That's tempting,'' Raider said, ''but I'm not the sort of fellow to sit still too long. If I did, I'd probably grow roots, and that's not right for somebody like me.''

''Will you come back to Salt Lake City?'' Molly asked.

''It's hard to say. Probably, but I never know if I'm going to be alive tomorrow, let alone where I'll be.''

''Please come back.''

''You'd better,'' said Ann, winking. ''I never did get to

spend quite as much time with you as I would have liked.''

"I promise you one thing," Raider said. "If I ever get anywhere near Salt Lake City again, you can bet I'm coming by and help you spend some of that money." He unfolded his long body from the sofa. "Now," he said, "it's time to go. Doc's waiting for me."

He hugged each of the brides until he reached Molly. He looked at her; she was crying.

"Why the tears?" he asked.

"I might never see you again."

He put his arms around her, picked her off the ground, and spun her around. "Don't worry about that, honey," he whispered in her ear. "I wouldn't miss the chance to see you all grown up."

He put her down, smiled, turned, and walked out the door. The girls rushed to windows and watched him mount his horse and ride out of sight.

Emily Stover put a cup of coffee down in front of Doc and then joined him on the sofa. She was quiet, preoccupied.

"What's wrong, Emily?" Doc asked.

"What do I have to show for all this? I know Clint was murdered, but that only makes me more angry and frustrated."

"I understand."

"No, Doc, I don't think you really do. You've solved your case. You've done what you came here for. You're satisfied. What am I?"

"A very beautiful lady."

"A very beautiful lady with nothing except memories of Clint and now memories of you."

"I have to move on, honey. It's my work. It's all I know."

"Doc, do you know that I didn't make love to a man

from the time Clint died until you came back into my life? I told myself I didn't need it, that it wasn't important. I told myself that Clint was the only man I could ever love.

"I know."

"But you changed that. You made me love you. You made me live, Doc, and now you're just going to walk out, and everything will be just like it was."

"What are you trying to say, Emily?"

"I'm asking you to stay, Doc. I'm asking you to make me your wife and to try to live a normal life for once. Neither one of us is as young as we used to be. Chances like this don't come along every day."

"Emily, I love you very much, but I'm not ready. It wouldn't work for either of us. You told me yourself that I shouldn't marry until I'm ready to settle down and live normal, until I've gotten Pinkerton out of my system. Well, that hasn't happened. I have to be honest with myself."

"Sometimes I talk too much, Doc." She dropped her head to his shoulder, and he put his arms around her.

"I just want you to know one thing, Emily," he said. "I'll miss you terribly. I've said that to a lot of women before, but this is one of the few times I really meant it. You made me feel things I've never felt before."

"I was only beginning."

"I know, and that's why I'm afraid to stay around for the end."

"Will I ever see you again?"

"You know Pinkerton. Maybe in a month, a year, five years. You never can tell."

"Yes, Doc, I know Pinkerton. I'm afraid I know it only too well."

They started to kiss as the door flew open and Raider walked in.

"Ooops," he said.

"Don't you ever knock?" Doc asked.

"Sorry, I wanted to show you this." He handed Doc a copy of that afternoon's newspaper.

Doc read the headline aloud: "James Gang Robs Provo Bank, Kills Two." He looked at Raider. "Don't worry," he said, "we'll have another chance at him. I know we will."

"I hope you do, Doc," Emily said. "I really hope you do." A tear rolled down her left cheek. She forced a smile, stood, and said brightly, "More coffee coming up!"

J.D. HARDIN

"THE MOST EXCITING WESTERN WRITER SINCE LOUIS L'AMOUR"

—JAKE LOGAN

_____	0-867-16840	BLOOD, SWEAT AND GOLD	$1.95
_____	0-867-16842	BLOODY SANDS	$1.95
_____	0-867-16882	BULLETS, BUZZARDS, BOXES OF PINE	$1.95
_____	0-867-16877	COLDHEARTED LADY	$1.95
_____	0-867-21101	DEATH FLOTILLA	$1.95
_____	0-867-16911	DEATH LODE	$1.95
_____	0-867-16843	FACE DOWN IN A COFFIN	$1.95
_____	0-867-16844	THE GOOD, THE BAD, AND THE DEADLY	$1.95
_____	0-867-21002	GUNFIRE AT SPANISH ROCK	$1.95
_____	0-867-16799	HARD CHAINS, SOFT WOMEN	$1.95
_____	0-867-16881	THE MAN WHO BIT SNAKES	$1.95
_____	0-867-16861	RAIDER'S GOLD	$1.95
_____	0-867-16883	RAIDER'S HELL	$1.95
_____	0-867-16767	RAIDER'S REVENGE	$1.95
_____	0-867-16839	SILVER TOMBSTONES	$1.95
_____	0-867-21133	SNAKE RIVER RESCUE	$1.95
_____	0-867-21039	SONS AND SINNERS	$1.95
_____	0-867-16869	THE SPIRIT AND THE FLESH	$1.95

 Berkley Book Mailing Service
P.O. Box 690, Rockville Centre, N.Y. 11570

Please send me the titles checked above. I enclose _____.
Include 75¢ for postage and handling if one book is ordered; 50¢ per book for
two to five. If six or more are ordered, postage is free. California, Illinois, New
York and Tennessee residents please add sales tax.

NAME _____

ADDRESS _____

CITY_____ STATE/ZIP_____.

Allow six weeks for delivery.